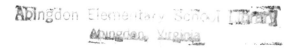

· Charlotte's Rose ·

A. E. CANNON

Charlotte's Rose

A Dell Yearling Book

F
Can

Published by
Dell Yearling
an imprint of
Random House Children's Books
a division of Random House, Inc.
New York

Visit us on the Web! www.randomhouse.com/kids

Educators and librarians, for a variety of teaching tools, visit us at www.randomhouse.com/teachers

ISBN: 0-440-41840-2

Reprinted by arrangement with Wendy Lamb Books

Printed in the United States of America

February 2004

10 9 8 7 6 5 4 3 2 1

OPM

7066

with love for my father,

LaVell Edwards,

who read this by the sea

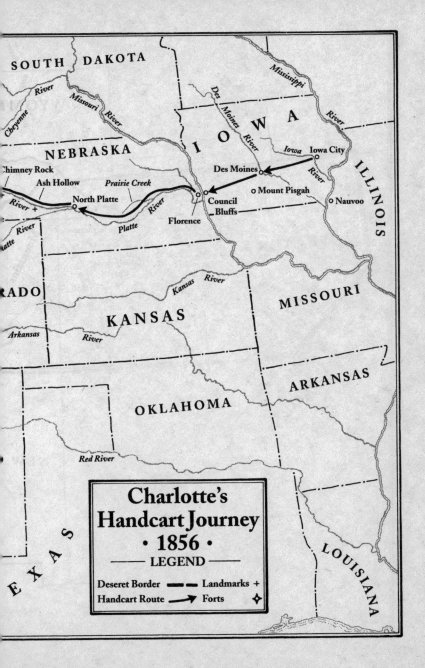

· Ocean ·

Saturday, April 19, 1856

❧

ABOARD THE *S. CURLING*, READY TO SET
SAIL FROM LIVERPOOL

Here's a secret I have not told a soul. Not even Papa.

I wish I were famous. Like Queen Victoria, maybe, although I would not care to look like her. She has lovely blue eyes, but she is too short.

So perhaps I would rather be famous like that man Dickens.

I am sure I could do what he does. Publish stories in journals and get paid. Oh, I have so many tales blooming in my head. Comedies. Romances. Tragedies. Some of them are stories Mam told me before she died, but most of them I just made up. I cut and stitched them from air.

My girlfriends back in Port Talbot, Wales, used to love my stories, especially the romances, which I told as we strolled through narrow streets at night. We walked to the Morfa Colliery to greet our fathers and brothers, who were covered with coal dust.

"How do you do it, Charlotte?" my friends would say.

Truly, I don't know. My head is just a cupboard. I open it up and the stories are waiting for me on the shelves.

So it is a huge sadness to me that although I will be thirteen years old come this summer, I cannot read. Nor can I write my stories down.

I must try to remember, then—everything that happens to us as Papa and I commence our journey this nineteenth day of April in the year of our Lord 1856 from the docks of Liverpool, England. Like those children of Israel who searched for the Promised Land, we are headed with seven hundred Mormon brothers and sisters for the distant blue mountains of Utah in America.

Zion!

I only pray that my remembrances will not unravel and turn back into air but will always hold their shapes in my heart.

Monday, April 21, 1856

∾

ON THE S. CURLING, IN CARDIGAN BAY, OFF THE WELSH COAST

Brother James Bowen sits across the chessboard from me, stroking his gray beard with strong fingers stained from years of scratching the earth for coal. Sister Margaret Bowen stands with her arms folded across her stout bosom, looking over her husband's shoulder. Papa rests on a stool nearby, carving a piece of wood. He's not wearing his hat, so his red hair gleams like copper in the sun.

We're surrounded by ship sounds. Sails snapping in the wind. Passengers gossiping. Children laughing. A band is playing "All Is Well" on the other side of the deck. One of the brothers from London is preaching in that language which I do *not* care for, but which I must learn because I'm going to America, where they speak English, not Welsh.

There are ship smells, too. Mingled scents of fish and food and wool clothing slightly wet. Papa teases me about my nose, saying I use it more than I use my ears or my eyes—or sometimes my head!

Brother Bowen reaches across the chessboard to make a move.

Just then I take a bite from my hard crust of bread and chew loudly.

Brother Bowen frowns. He draws his hand back as if he has just touched something hot. Sister Bowen catches my eye and winks. She understands what is happening here, of course. Sister Bowen understands everything.

Overhead a circle of seagulls laughs against a bright blue sky. Inside, I laugh with them. *Ha! Ha! Ha! I am beating you for the first time ever in my whole life, Brother Bowen.*

"Good afternoon, President and Sister Bowen. Brother Edwards."

Oh no.

It's that awful old Brother Nathaniel Roberts and his shriveled wife, Lititia, who believe they are more righteous than the rest of us. They come from Glamorgan County like the Bowens and Papa and me, although Brother Roberts didn't work in the mines.

They used to have money once. You can tell because

of the expensive cameo Sister Roberts always wears pinned beneath her chin.

I was hoping we could leave the Robertses behind in Wales.

"Good afternoon, Nathaniel. Lititia," says Papa.

Sister Bowen smiles and nods, though her smile is more polite than friendly. Brother Bowen is too busy scowling at my rook to say hello.

Brother and Sister Roberts pretend to stroll about the deck enjoying the brisk sea air, but they have come to spy. Last night after evening prayers, I overheard them telling handsome Brother George Jenkins and his beautiful wife, Rosa, that playing chess was the first step toward gambling, and that they were disappointed in Brother Bowen. Imagine, they said, a church leader teaching a wild little girl like Charlotte Edwards to play a game like *that*.

At first their words made me quiver inside, the way I always do when I realize someone is angry with me again. I don't mean to cause trouble. But then I got mad at Brother and Sister Roberts.

For one thing, I am not a little girl. Mam died at Christmastime giving birth to my brother David. He also died. Since then I have kept house for my father, Daniel Edwards, a collier and pit carpenter.

For another, chess and gambling are *not* the same thing, although I may take up gambling one day just to irritate Brother and Sister Roberts.

Anyway, Brother Roberts is jealous of Brother Bowen, who was made president of our group yesterday in a general meeting of all seven hundred Mormons on board. (The rest of the passengers on the *S. Curling* are gentiles, meaning they are not Mormons.) We were divided into eleven groups, or wards, in which to conduct our worship and to help one another with cooking and cleaning on our voyage. Papa and I are in the Bowens' ward.

Sister Roberts gives a dry snort. She and Brother Roberts link arms and leave.

Dear God, I say in my head, *please bless that the two of them will lose their footing and slip. Soon.*

Brother Bowen cocks a bushy brow. "Your daughter seems to think she has me trapped, Daniel."

Papa smiles. Brother Bowen growls at me.

"You do not scare me, Brother Bowen," I say, taking another noisy bite of bread. "But then, you do not scare anybody."

"Our Charlotte speaks the truth, Husband." Sister Bowen rumples Brother Bowen's hair as if he is a clumsy puppy tumbling at her feet.

"Daniel, you really must teach your daughter to respect her elders," grumbles Brother Bowen. "Also, I would appreciate it if you would encourage her to chew with her mouth shut, especially when she is playing chess with me."

Papa and Sister Bowen and I whoop with laughter.

And so do the seagulls, which spin like angels on white wings above us.

Brother Bowen makes his move.

And I make mine. "Check."

Boom!

Ocean water shoots straight up from the sea and sprays everyone on this end of the deck. I blink. My hair is soaked and my clothes are plastered to my skin. The chess pieces crash to the floor and roll beneath our feet.

"Lordy!" says Sister Bowen as she shakes drops of water from her hands.

Someone laughs.

I look up and see the Bowens' son John grinning down from the top of Captain Curling's cabin, where he sits, lazily swinging his long legs, which are not at all wet. His hair stands straight up in the wind like a glossy black coxcomb.

His eyes catch mine, and he smirks at me.

I fling my half-eaten crust at his head. He dodges it easily.

"That's enough, Charlotte! And you," Brother Bowen shouts at John, "get down from there right now."

John reddens, and it's as though we are six and seven years old again, being scolded for chasing each other around Sister Bowen's table. We used to be great friends when we were small, although I can scarcely believe it now.

John leaps to the deck and stoops to gather up our

chess pieces, which he places back on the board. Except for my king, which he casually stuffs into his pocket.

"Check, Charlotte."

"Give it back to me. Now."

John pulls out the king and flips it through the air to me. Then he saunters off.

Brother Bowen frowns as he watches John go. "He is so different from our other sons, Margaret."

John's brothers, Evan and Thomas Bowen, chose to stay behind in Wales with their own families for now. Brother Bowen's eyes grow wet whenever he speaks of them.

"Something is troubling that boy," he says to Sister Bowen.

"Something has been troubling that boy ever since he started working in the colliery," she says.

I look after John as he walks away.

Troubled? Oh, I think not.

Wicked, perhaps.

What could be troubling wicked, teasing John Bowen?

Tuesday, April 22, 1856

❧

OFF THE WEXFORD COAST OF IRELAND

The sea is bright and calm today. And boring. I suppose I'm the only passenger who hopes for the drama of a good windstorm.

"George! No!"

I turn just in time to see Rosa Jenkins swoop down upon her baby son as he strays near the side of the ship. She bundles him up in her arms and covers his hair with kisses.

"No, no, no, Georgie!"

I sigh.

Not that I want anybody to go overboard. Still . . .

A rogue wave crashes over the side of the ship, sweeping

someone—a child, an old person with a crutch, Captain Curling's terrier, it doesn't matter who—out to sea.

There is no time to spare.

I climb onto this railing and leap straight into the icy water.

Later, Captain Curling assembles everyone on the deck and asks me to give a speech.

I pull my shawl tight around my shoulders, spin around, and wander as if in a dream toward the rear of the boat.

And I almost step on something.

It looks like a bit of blanket—tiny squares of cloth pieced together like a quilt for a fairy.

I bend over to pick it up and discover a small doll bundled inside.

Such a doll!

I trail my finger across the doll's cool china face. I wanted a doll exactly like this one when I was younger. Black haired. Gray eyed. Cheeks like pink roses. I lift up the doll's green gingham skirt and see that she has green boots painted on her dainty porcelain feet.

I had a doll of my own once. I made her from the sole of a worn-out shoe, and I called her Ann after one of Mam's babies. I used to bundle my shoe doll in rags and take her to bed with me every night. Mam would tell me a story, and then she would tell Ann a story, too.

It always made me smile to hear Mam talk to Ann as if she were a real little girl.

So I loved my shoe doll. But *this* doll, with the soft body and the china head, was the one I truly wanted.

Slowly, carefully, I wrap up the doll and try to imagine its owner. A girl, of course. Seven or eight years old. Richer than we are if her family can afford a doll like this—

Someone is watching me. I feel it.

I whirl around to find a woman with an angry red scar across the left side of her face. Our eyes meet just as a violent gust of wind shoots across the deck, swirling her black skirts around her legs and whipping her loose black hair across her face. If she were to spread open her shawl at this moment, she would fly straight to the top of the billowing white sails!

I swallow hard. This woman has been watching me since the day Papa and I boarded the ship. I'm not imagining it, either, although it's true I sometimes imagine things.

"Who is that woman?" I asked Sister Bowen last night as we cleared our dishes.

"Catherine Jones," said Sister Bowen. "James's brother Richard baptized her in Liverpool last spring. She was living alone, working as a seamstress. She is Welsh like us."

"What's she like?"

"Extremely clever. I've seen her steal away to write in a journal when she thinks no one is watching." Sister Bowen paused and smiled a little. "It would make interesting reading if I could read. And if she cared to share it with me. I suspect she doesn't miss much of what's going on around her."

"Are you her friend?" I asked.

"I'm as much of a friend to her as she'll let me be, Charlotte. She keeps her distance from other people, does our Catherine Jones."

"Why?"

"She has reasons which make sense to her." Sister Bowen shrugged.

"What are they?"

"It's not for me to say. Most likely you're too young to understand them anyway. Now, hand me those mugs there, and let's speak of something else."

Sister Bowen's comment that I am too young to understand still stings as I look at Catherine Jones now. Why do her eyes follow me? Does she mean me harm?

I tuck the doll beneath my shawl. For some reason, I don't want this woman to know what I have found.

"Good morning, Sister Jones." I sound brave, which is good.

"Good morning," she says in a cool voice. *"Charlotte."*

"You know my name?" I squeak.

"Oh, I think you would be surprised at the things I know." She brushes the hair from her face and looks at the bundle in my arms.

Guilt shoots through me. I turn and walk away on limp legs, clutching my hidden doll.

Now, why should I feel guilty? I haven't stolen this doll. I'm not keeping her for myself. I'll find the little girl who owns her and hand it back to her before this day is over.

Just see if I don't, Catherine Jones!

I am so hungry tonight.

We had chicken for supper, which was very nice, although it did make me somewhat sick to stand in the kitchen earlier today with a group of children and watch the cooks wring the necks of those poor birds.

I wasn't filled, however, even though I ate all my food, then crunched on the chicken bones afterward. So my stomach is growling, which makes me angry with John for causing me to throw my bread at him yesterday. I would like to have that bit of crust to chew on now.

It's John's fault that I am hungry.

My stomach grumbles again. A man sitting two rows ahead of me turns to stare at me instead of listening to Brother Nathaniel Roberts, droning on and on and on about the prophet Joseph Smith as our ward sits shivering together on the deck for evening prayers and songs and preaching.

Truly, if I had a stone, I'd throw it at Brother Roberts's thick head for taking the story about Joseph Smith and making it as dull as dirt.

It's a thrilling story, if you know how to tell it right. A fourteen-year-old American boy goes into the woods to pray about which church he should join, and God tells him to create a brand-new one instead. When he is a young man, an angel in flowing white robes leads him to the side of a green mountain and shows him ancient pages made of gold, which Joseph translates into the Book of Mormon.

People read his book and listen to him preach, and some of them believe him, although his story makes other people very angry. They think he is a liar and a thief. So Joseph is finally killed under the cover of night by a mob of men who hate him and the other Mormons, too.

His church does not die with him, though.

Brigham Young, a practical prophet who is often called the Lion of the Lord, takes over like Moses and leads Joseph's followers out of Nauvoo, Illinois, to a distant Rocky Mountain desert. Zion. The Promised Land. The place where Mormons have been commanded like the Children of Israel to gather and build his kingdom here on Earth so we can work and worship safely there.

Most of us—Welsh, English, Scotch, a few Irish—traveling aboard the *S. Curling* are too poor to afford this journey. But Brother Brigham and the others in Salt Lake City have raised money and sent it to us to make our voyage possible. I hear that Brother Brigham is a lively prophet who loves to square-dance and to sing.

Oh, I do like the story of Joseph Smith very much, especially the beginning when he's just fourteen. It's sweet to think that God would look down from heaven and bother with a boy who was only a little older than John, kneeling among the trees. But Brother Roberts is boring me to tears.

So I am grumpy *and* hungry.

I take some comfort in the secret doll that is tucked beneath my arm, even though I am far too old for dolls.

I sigh. I know I should have looked for the little girl who owns her. I meant to. First after lunch. Then after supper. But I couldn't bear to part with her today. I'll find the doll's true owner tomorrow.

Papa slides his arm across my shoulders and pulls me close to him. He's warm, and I adore the way his jacket smells, like wood shavings and smoke. Papa perfume.

I don't mind Brother Roberts now that I am wrapped up in Papa's arms. It's always a miracle to me, the way my father loves me even when I don't love myself.

The boat rocks us like she is our mam and we are her children. I look up at the chilly night sky and see an old friend. Polaris. The North Star. The axis that the rest of the sky turns around like the wheel of a wagon.

Mam showed me how to find Polaris when I was little. Locate the Plow—or the Big Dipper, as some people call it. Look at the far right side of the Plow. Draw a line in your head between the bottom star and top star, then extend your imaginary line five times and you will be at your journey's end.

Mam loved the stars. The moon, too, which looks down upon us this evening like a white shining face.

Mam, are you still watching over Papa and me?

The answer comes back in a whisper of wind.

Oh yes. Always.

Brother Roberts continues to speak. There is spittle on his lower lip. I look away.

I'll make up the kind of story that Mam used to tell me and the shoe doll, Ann, and the people in our group will be my characters. I snuggle closer to Papa.

There'll be a wicked witch in my story, and an evil giant who laughs as he grinds the bones of men as easily as I grind chicken bones between my teeth. I'll put in fairies full of magic. And of course, a princess and her prince.

First the witch. I spy Sister Roberts sitting in the front row, fingering the cameo at her neck.

She never stops touching that cameo. Sometimes I even see her gazing in one of the ship's mirrors at it. Right now she gazes with pride at her husband.

Can it be she doesn't realize how much he tortures the rest of us? Can she truly *love* him even though he has hair sprouting from each ear?

Sister Roberts would certainly make an excellent witch. She even has a small wart on her chin. But then, so does Sister Bowen, an even bigger wart. And Sister Bowen is handsome.

I notice Catherine Jones, with the scarred crimson face, sitting apart from the rest of us. She plucks at her shawl with long slender fingers and looks as bored as I feel.

I could almost like her at this minute. Then I remember the way she made me shiver this morning. So. Catherine Jones will be my witch.

Slap, slap, slap . . .

If I weren't so interested in my story, the sound of waves slapping our ship's sides would lure me to my dreams.

Now for the evil giant. John has grown five inches since last summer. I steal a look at him lounging in the ship's shadows and discover that he's already looking at me. He grins like a devil and shoots me a slow wink.

Oh! I wish I had that crust to throw at him all over again!

Now the fairies.

Slap, slap . . .

My fairies are three Welsh girls close to my own age.

The shortest one has fair hair and a beautiful singing voice. The second girl is as plain and plump as a soft brown hen, and she has a jolly laugh. The third girl is quiet and pretty with eyes the color of spring leaves.

They are all named Elizabeth. Which makes me very happy indeed that I am called Charlotte.

I hope that the three Elizabeths and I will be friends, especially now that I do not care for John.

Slap . . .

And now for my princess and her prince. There's Ellenor Roberts, who is loud and lively and in love with young Elias Lewis, who I'm sure loves her back. They're sitting on opposite ends of a row right now, stealing glances at each other. First Ellenor looks at Elias. Then Elias looks at Ellenor. Oh! They're looking at each other at the same time! Elias blushes. Ellenor grins.

Ellenor is neat and proud of her shoes, which I often see her shining on the ship's deck. I like her very much. But she does not look like a princess, mostly because of the strawberry-colored freckles that stretch across her face and arms like fields of tiny poppies.

Sister Rosa Jenkins, the woman who rescued Georgie, could be my princess, with her white skin and soft eyes and moon-colored hair wound around her head like a crown. Her husband, George, is handsome, too. So are Georgie and baby Emma, who still nurses. Brother and Sister Jenkins sit close and trade kisses when they think no one is watching.

But the woman I want to be my princess is this one sitting in front of me and Papa. Her name is Mary Owen, and she looks like Mam did when Mam was pregnant. I love the way her heavy dark hair covers her shoulders at night after we say our prayers and crawl into our berths.

Her husband, Thomas, with the strong shoulders like Papa's, will be the prince of the story, which will end happily ever after.

Oh, this will be a fine tale. My girlfriends in Port Talbot would love this tale. If only I could write it down.

Brother Roberts finishes speaking. Hallelujah! I stretch out my legs. Papa heaves a yawn, then smiles sheepishly.

And now a blind man picks his way to the front of our group, assisted by a young woman, who seats him and then brings him a harp.

Papa whispers in my ear. "That is Brother Thomas Giles, Charlotte. They say he has converted many Welsh souls to Mormonism."

"What happened to him?" I ask, watching Brother Giles place his hands on the strings, preparing to play.

"He lost his eyesight in a terrible mining accident." Papa's face grows grim. "I give thanks to God every night that did not happen to me when I worked in the colliery."

Brother Giles touches the harp's strings, and music, sad and sweet, surrounds us. The sea swings us to and fro, and I am filled with a deep yearning I don't understand.

"He plays like an angel, does our Brother Giles," says Papa into my hair.

"Ay-eeee!" Sister Roberts leaps up and hops from foot to foot. "A rat! A rat! A rat just ran across my shoes!"

I start to laugh so hard that I fear I will crack my ribs. John laughs, and we look at each other across the sea of heads and hats between us, enjoying the spectacle of Sister Roberts dancing. John and I have always laughed at the same things.

Dear God, I say in my head, *I know I asked you to make Sister Roberts slip and fall on the deck. But a rat is a much better idea.*

Thank you.

Wednesday, April 23, 1856

❦

AT SEA

Brother Bowen, John, and I are sitting together on the deck enjoying the sun, which warms us in spite of the cold sea air.

I have the doll still. She's tucked tight beneath my clothes. I plan to look for her owner this afternoon. Meanwhile, I must keep her hidden from John or he'll tease me and say I'm too old for dolls.

I am. Truly, I do not understand why I still cling to this china girl.

Meanwhile, the three of us are listening to one of the ship's sailors, a white-whiskered, one-legged gentile. I must ask him what happened to his other leg. I'm sure it's quite a story. Right now he's telling us about the time he spent in America, working on the railroads and fighting Indians.

"You have a long journey ahead of you," the sailor says. "The prairie stretches on forever."

We'll ride a train to a place called Iowa City, where our group of seven hundred people will be divided into smaller companies. Each family will be outfitted with a handcart in which to carry their belongings. And then we will pull our handcarts to Utah.

It will be hard work, but I'm unnaturally strong for a scrawny girl. Perhaps I'll even grow up to be as strong as Sister Bowen, who used to work in the mines pulling trams up from the pit, even though it was illegal for a woman to be there.

Will our cart be like the kind used by street vendors to sell fruits and vegetables and flowers? How heavy will it be with our things loaded in it? Can Papa and I really push it all the way across America?

My stomach skitters.

"What does the prairie look like?" I ask.

The sailor shuts his eyes, remembering. "Like the ocean. Especially when the wind blows through the grass. I stood on a railroad track at the prairie's edge one night when the sun was setting and grew homesick for the sea."

He opens his eyes and winks at me. "You will see buffalo there."

"Buffalo?"

"Great ugly cow creatures with large heads and

shaggy beards. They thunder in herds across the great plains. Thousands of them. When they run, they look like a moving mountain. The Indians kill them for meat."

John gazes across the prairie of water before us, his face thoughtful.

"Are there snakes in America?" One of the things I hate most in this world is snakes, with their flicking tongues and the way they slither and slide and look at you with glittering secret eyes.

"America is a big country," says the sailor. "Lots of room for snakes there. Especially in the desert, where you're going."

I grasp the railing, and my hair flaps in the wind as I remember a scrap of Scripture.

"And the desert shall rejoice, and blossom as the rose!"

Which is very nice, since that is where we're going. But why do snakes have to be there, too?

"And what can you tell us about the wolves that live in America?" John asks.

I know he's thinking of the song a passenger taught us last night, about a group of Mormon soldiers—the Mormon Battalion—that marched across America to fight against the Spanish. I've already learned the first verse by heart.

The Mormons were camped down by the green grove
Where the clear waters flow from the mountains
above.

The wind it approached, all chilly and cold,
And we listened to the howling of those lonesome
  roving wolves.

Such a stirring song. Even better than Brother Bowen's famous ghost stories. Just thinking about the song and the way it was sung last night on the deck of the ship, with the water rolling and the wind moaning, gives me the chills right now.

I could tell John liked the song, too.

Here's a secret. Sometimes I sneak glances at John and study the way he moves, which is different and strange to me now that his legs have sprouted. I note the way his voice has changed, as well as the expressions he wears when he thinks no one is watching him.

I'm not sure why I do this, because I truly dislike him.

So I looked at John last night, with the evening shadows dancing across his dark face, and I saw him grow still and thoughtful when people talked about the bravery of those soldiers.

"Indeed, there are wolves in America," says the sailor.

"But then, there are wolves in Wales, too," says Brother Bowen. "English landlords and anglified Welsh industrialists."

The sailor's lips stretch into a dark grin. "Who live in hillside mansions with windows that look down on the factories and docks and mines where men like us work."

Brother Bowen shakes his head. "And pay salaries in tokens that can be used only in the stores that they own."

Though he does not speak of it now, Brother Bowen rode with the Rebecca rioters when he was young. They were a group of Welsh workingmen who put on women's clothes and blackened their faces with soot, then stormed through the countryside of Glamorgan at night, destroying tollgates because people were being taxed to death by the English.

Things will be so different in Utah. We'll have our own land, and I'll grow two rosebushes in front of our new cottage there—pink roses for me, red for Mam.

"Just remember this," the sailor says to Brother Bowen, "Wales was Wales before England was even dreamed of."

Brother Bowen roars out a mighty laugh.

"Husband, I need you!" Sister Bowen lunges toward us. Three days on the water, and she still has not adjusted to the ship's motion. "Our bags have tumbled out of our berth. I'm so seasick I topple over when I try to pick them up."

"John. Charlotte. Do not plague each other while I am gone." Brother Bowen heaves an exaggerated sigh and leaves.

The sailor suddenly shoots out his arm and jabs a finger into the air. "Look! Out there! A mermaid!"

John snorts as I scramble to my feet and hang so far over the railing that sea spray washes my face.

"Where?" I am breathless.

"Keep looking," the sailor says.

"Have you seen lots of mermaids?" I ask.

"Hundreds," he says. "If you hold out a mirror, they'll swim to the side of the ship and look in it. They're vain creatures with glossy hair the length of a horse's tail."

I keep searching the gleaming sea. I want to see the mermaid as much as I want to see buffalo in America.

"There'll be a mighty storm tonight," the sailor crows. "A storm always follows the sighting of a mermaid. You wait and see."

"John! I can see her head!"

At least it looks like a head out there, bobbing among the waves.

And why should it not be the head of a mermaid? Mam always said the world is wide and full of wonders.

Or at least that is what I *think* she said. Sometimes I wonder if I have her words right.

Time for dinner soon.

I tried to help in the kitchen when it was our ward's shift, but I spilled a kettle of tea on the floor and knocked a bowl off the table, which made all the sisters cross with me.

So I have stolen away to this spot here at the rear of the *S. Curling* to be by myself.

Not that one can be truly alone on this ship. But at least I'm not surrounded by people who remind me that I'm a child who's in the way.

Yesterday I could still see a bit of land from this spot. Today there's just a bright red sun sinking into the ocean.

"Your name is Charlotte, isn't it?" Sister Mary Owen joins me.

I nod. How nice—she knows who I am.

Sister Owen's walk is slow and graceful. She grasps the rail with the right hand and holds her swelling belly with the left. I try to remember all the times that Mam looked just like her. Mam had six babies. I was the first. The only one who lived.

Sister Owen gives me a faint smile. "Are you as seasick as I am?"

"Papa lost his breakfast this morning. So did Sister Bowen. But I have not felt the least bit ill."

"You're like my Thomas. A natural born sailor. He hasn't been sick, either." Sister Owen's face grows glad when she says her husband's name.

"When is your baby coming, Sister Owen?"

If Papa were here, he would knit his shaggy red brows together and shake his head at me for being too forward.

Sister Owen gives me a startled look. Then she laughs and I grin back at her.

"This summer, Sister Charlotte. Thomas and our baby and I will join his sister's family in Utah. I know they will welcome this child."

"Where do they live?"

"In Cedar City, several hundred miles south of Salt Lake."

"We're going north to Ogden with the Bowens, who have family there," I say, disappointed that Sister Owen and I will live so far apart. Utah, which is only a portion of America, is much bigger than Wales. We will probably never see each other again after our journey is over.

Sister Owen pulls her shawl tight around her shoulders and gazes across the swelling ocean to the spot where we last saw land. Her eyes narrow, and the expression on her sweet face changes.

"Goodbye, Wales," she says in a sudden angry whisper. "Goodbye to my Thomas dropped deep into the mines each morning. Goodbye to waiting for him to return."

The ship lists gently, and I place my hand on the railing next to hers. She has small pretty hands—just like Mam.

"Goodbye to washing coal dust from Papa's clothes," I say, thinking of Mam's hands working. My hands, too.

"Goodbye to washing coal dust from my Thomas's hair."

"Goodbye to sweeping coal dust from the floor."

A gull dips and laughs overhead. Sister Owen and I grin at our new game.

"Goodbye to rain every day," she says.

"Goodbye to mud after rain every day," I say.

"Goodbye to narrow valleys," she says.

"Goodbye to narrow valley streets," I say.

"Goodbye to boys kicking pig bladders down narrow valley streets," she says.

"Goodbye to shrieking girls chasing boys kicking pig bladders down narrow valley streets," I say.

Sister Owen throws back her head and laughs. So do I.

"Charlotte, you make me forget that I am seasick. Oh, thank you!"

Her words turn my cheeks pink. I know Sister Owen and I will be great friends even though she's a woman and I'm a girl.

Sister Owen grabs the railing with both hands. She stands, feet apart, and turns her head to look at me. "I will say one last goodbye now, Charlotte. To my mother. Who turned her back on me when I joined with the Mormons."

She looks eastward and shouts as the wind blows back her thick dark hair. "You have your wish now, Mam. I am gone. *Ffarwel!*"

Her voice drops to a whisper. "You will not see me in this life again, I think."

Sister Owen's words send shivers chasing up my arms.

Pots rattle. Pans jump. Bags hop about like clumsy rabbits. A tin box from an upper berth crashes to the floor. Women groan and babies whimper. Elizabeth the Musical sings to her small brother, who cries.

I am surrounded by crazy music this evening as wind and rain and sea pound the sides of our poor ship.

Sister Bowen lets out a mighty, bed-shaking oath. Sister Roberts would be shocked to hear her if she were sharing this berth with us tonight. Luckily she is not. But Catherine Jones is.

They have stuck me in the middle of them like butter between halves of a biscuit.

"Catherine!" shouts Sister Bowen. "I am going to be ill again!"

Sister Bowen rolls out of bed. The ship lurches and sways. Sister Bowen vomits before she can reach one of the pans we have set out.

Catherine Jones crawls over me. She crouches on the floor and cleans up while Sister Bowen covers her mouth with her fist.

I flop over and bury my nose in our bed as it pitches to and fro. I pull Mam's quilt over my head.

I dearly love Sister Bowen, even though she does not believe me when I tell her she snores. But I have no desire to smell her dinner a second time tonight.

Oh! Oh! *Oh!*

How I wish this boat would stop its endless heaving.

Oh, I am ill.

Mam, I miss you. I want you.

Here's something I'm learning. People forget things. Even if they swore they would never *ever* forget, no matter what. Forgetting what another person was like is easy.

How she held her head when she listened to you.

How she laughed when you told her a riddle you had just made up.

How her skin felt and especially how it smelled like

rose water when she held you tight in her arms each night as the moon rose outside your tiny streaked window.

How she took your fingers and kissed them. One by one by one.

At first my memories of Mam were so real I could almost see her kneeling in her favorite spot by the fire. See her look up and smile as I walked into the room.

The days passed.

The months, too.

Then one morning I discovered that while I could still see her kneeling there just like she always did, I couldn't quite make out the details of her face.

But oh, I did remember her hands this afternoon when Sister Owen gripped the railing.

I reach beneath my pillow and find the secret doll there. I rub the top of her beautiful china hair as a story appears in my head.

Once upon a time there was a little girl who lost her favorite doll while sailing to America. She loved the beautiful doll with the gingham dress and the green boots, and she looked all over the ship for her.

But she did not find her.

One day a sailor spotted a mermaid in the distance and warned the passengers that there would be a terrible storm. That night the waves reached up like cat paws and batted the boat about.

The little girl was lonely and afraid. She was sick with yearning for the company of her doll. . . .

I don't always like my own stories, frankly.

I touch the doll's pink cheek one last time, then tuck her beneath my pillow. Of all the wicked things I've done and said and thought since leaving Liverpool four days ago, hiding this doll has been the most wicked.

You cannot keep a thing that isn't freely given.

Thursday, April 24, 1856

❧

At Sea

I've certainly tried to find the doll's owner.

You'd think that someone would have heard something about a lost doll. But no.

I've asked and I've asked.

The ocean sparkles in the sun like a field of crystals, so bright it hurts my eyes. Kicking at a stray potato peel dropped on the deck, I drag toward the spot where I first found this china lady. There are two girls standing there, both younger than I am. Sisters. They have the same ash-colored curls springing from beneath their bonnets, the same fair skin dusted with ash-colored freckles. I can tell from their clothes that they're Welsh.

"Excuse me," I say. "I found a doll here the other day, and I'm looking for her owner."

Both girls stare at me openmouthed.

"You have her?" the younger one asks.

Suddenly I'm short of breath. My hand shakes as I reach for the doll tucked in the crook of my arm, covered by my shawl. "Is this yours?" I hold the doll in front of me.

The sisters squeal and clap their hands.

"Oh, thank you!" the older one breathes. She takes the doll and cradles her. "Priscilla—that's what we call her— was a special gift to us when we left."

"I just set her down for a moment to chase Captain Curling's dog the other day," the other sister says. "When I came back here, she was gone."

"We didn't dare say anything to anyone 'cause we'd be in terrible trouble. Mam was suspicious, though. Last night she asked why we hadn't been playing with Priscilla." The older one smiles at her sister, then hands her the doll. The little sister kisses the top of Priscilla's head.

Even though I don't feel like smiling, I do. We chatter like ocean birds about Priscilla, the captain's dog, the storm last night, the ship's food. Then they thank me again and rush off.

Goodbye, I say in my head, already missing the feeling of cool china skin beneath my fingers.

· *City* ·

Monday, May 26, 1856

❧

IN BOSTON, BOARDING A TRAIN BOUND
FOR IOWA CITY

Whistles scream. Papa shouts as he slides a bag across the platform and stacks it next to the trunk where I'm perched.

"This is the last of our things. The train'll be here soon."

I nod at Papa as I stuff stray hair beneath my deadly plain bonnet. The best thing you can say about this bonnet is that it's not as ugly as my other one.

Papa rests his hand on my shoulder. "Are you happier today?"

"Happy to be leaving Boston," I grumble.

Papa grins. "But Boston's a grand place, full of fine buildings and interesting sights." He gives me a squeeze.

"Forget about what happened on the docks the other morning, Daughter. It's passed now."

I shrug and look down the tracks for a first glimpse of the train that will haul us to the frontier Mormon camp outside of Iowa City.

As I keep watch, I remember the sick feeling I had inside when the woman on the wharf began to cry.

Why is it that the things you don't want to remember stay with you like the throb of a toothache?

I was standing at the railing with Elizabeth the Jolly when we first saw Cape Ann four days ago. The next day the tugboat *Enoch Train* greeted us and towed us into Boston Bay, where we were quarantined to make sure we did not bring disease with us. We couldn't leave the ship until inspectors had boarded and examined us.

We passed the time on deck, packed and sweltering, beneath a field of hot sky, wishing for the feel of solid city beneath our feet.

At last the quarantine doctor said we were free to go. Sister Bowen, who understands English, heard him say we were a very clean people, which made me laugh, since Sister Roberts is always scolding me for being so messy.

By the morning of the twenty-fourth, I was eager to leave the ship and join the crowd of noisy strangers on the docks below. Americans! Most of them were women with neat little parasols. But there were men, too, some of them wearing ministers' frocks.

"Who are all these people?" I asked Sister Bowen, my stomach fluttering with excitement. "Have they come to welcome us to Boston?"

Sister Bowen's face was flat, like a mask. "We'll see."

A mighty cheer erupted on deck as the gangplank was finally lowered. We all crowded off the boat, bumping and jostling one another as we went. Papa and the Bowens were in front of me, the Robertses and Catherine Jones behind. Just ahead I spotted the sisters whose doll I'd returned. The younger one was clutching Priscilla and laughing.

I thought unless I gripped on to the tail of Papa's jacket, I would float away with happiness.

Then I saw *her* standing there on the wharf.

Actually, I saw her bonnet. Dove gray trimmed with lavender bows and ruffles and tiny silk flowers. I touched my own.

Dear God, I wouldn't mind having a hat like that *upon my head when I walk across the prairie. Thank you.*

The woman gave me a kind smile and an elegant wave.

I smiled back and began a new story.

"Hello," the lovely young woman said. *"My name is Amanda and I am your first new friend in America. Let me take you for a ride in my carriage and show you the sights of Boston, after which we will toss your dreary bonnet to the wind and buy you a new hat. . . ."*

As I approached, she said something to me in English as she tried to hand me a pamphlet.

I hesitated. I didn't want to offend her, but what would a Welsh girl do with her American pamphlet?

I looked at her face again and saw her sympathetic blue eyes fill with sudden tears.

I frowned.

Why was she crying?

The woman smiled at me again in spite of her tears and tried to hand me the pamphlet again. She nodded so vigorously that the lavender ribbon beneath her pretty chin trembled. Confused, I finally took it.

"*Diolch*."

I thanked her, then stuffed it into my pocket and ran to catch up with Papa.

Just then one of our leaders, Dan Jones, stood on a platform of crates and addressed the Americans on the wharf in English. We stood back and listened while Sister Bowen translated.

"Thank you for welcoming us to your beautiful city," he said. "Thank you, too, for your heartfelt charitable efforts to steer the less faithful among us away from Mormonism with your tracts and your pamphlets. You have my blessings in this endeavor because we cannot afford to carry the uncommitted with us on the long difficult journey to Utah."

Surprised laughter rippled through the crowd.

"Meanwhile, if any of you noble Bostonians has the desire to know more about the word of God, I will be preaching upon the wharf tomorrow morning at eleven o'clock. . . ."

Papa and Brother Bowen smiled.

"He's a sly one, that Elder Jones," said Brother Bowen.

As for me, I slid my hand into my pocket and touched the pamphlet there, wondering if those surprising tears had been for me.

I finally looked at the pamphlet when Papa and I shared a picnic with the Bowens near Bunker Hill, a place Brother Bowen wanted to see because the Americans had once fought the British there.

There was a drawing on one of the pages that caught my eye. It was of a large rooster with a hideous human head. The rooster was surrounded by a flock of hens, each with the head of a vicious-looking woman. The hens were screeching and pecking at their own chicks, which had the faces of spoiled children.

I puzzled over the drawing.

Who were these unnatural creatures? Why had the woman on the docks given me this?

I showed John the drawing. "What does it mean?"

Red splotches appeared on his sea-rough cheeks as he studied it.

"It's a picture of us. Mormons. People here think we're animals."

"Really?" My voice seeped out of me.

John shot me a look of contempt. "Stop being stupid. The only place we won't be odd is in Utah."

I looked at the drawing again. Then I glanced around and imagined that everyone in the whole beautiful city of Boston was staring at us. I felt myself shrink in their sight, as though I had swallowed an evil potion.

John wadded the pamphlet into a ball and pitched it hard into a pond, where ducks, thinking he had thrown them a bit of bread, scrambled to snap it up.

Later that night as we prepared to turn into our berths on the *S. Curling*—the captain was kind enough to let us stay there until we left by rail for Iowa City—Papa asked me what was wrong.

"You've been sulking all day," he teased.

So I told him about the lady in the dove gray bonnet and the pamphlet with the picture.

"She smiled at me, Papa," I said. "I thought she was kind."

"I'm sure she is. I suspect she was trying to rescue you and the other sisters."

"Why?" I felt my neck prickle. I can rescue myself.

"People object to the way some Mormon men have more than one wife. They don't understand it."

I scrunched up my face. "Well, I don't understand it, either."

"Neither do I, Charlotte." Papa smiled a little, then searched the evening sky as though he might find secret answers tucked there among the stars. "I haven't thought about plural marriage much. I didn't need to because no one practiced it in Wales." He sighed. "All I really know is that Joseph Smith preached we should try to live like the prophets of old in every way."

"Do you want to live like a prophet of old when we get to Utah?"

Papa looked so horrified I burst out laughing.

"Your mam could have, perhaps. She was so strong, Charlotte. Once she found it, her faith was fiery and fierce. But as much as I loved her, we were different people."

Papa and I sat without speaking for a while as the ship softly rocked and Boston Bay sang us a watery lullaby. I saw him smile to himself.

"What are you thinking about?" I asked.

"Remember how your mam tried to get us both to memorize Scripture the way she did?"

I smiled a little, too. "Yes."

"I'm afraid they didn't stick with me the way they did with her. I have more skill with wood than words. But I do remember this from the Bible: 'Again, the kingdom of heaven is like unto a net, that was cast into the sea, and gathered of every kind.' "

He dropped a kiss on my hair before standing to go to his bedroll on the deck.

"I believe that God allows for differences in his children," he whispered. "Even in Zion."

Another whistle blows. I wish it would blast the memory of that horrible drawing from my head. Every time I think of it, I feel as if I am only a scrap of the person I used to be.

Who drew it?

Didn't the artist realize a Mormon girl might see it one day and feel hurt?

Or was that what he wanted?

"Charlotte! Brother Edwards!" It's Mary Owen and her husband, Thomas, come to join us on the platform. She gives me a little hug, and I feel her growing baby between us.

I hope it's a girl.

A huge train lumbers up the tracks toward us, belching smoke. Railway workers appear and begin sliding open massive doors. They bark orders at us in English. People load their possessions.

I stand frozen. "We're going to Iowa City in these, Papa?"

He nods as he passes a piece of luggage up to Brother Owen, who already stands inside the car.

"They say the trip will take eight days if we travel both day and night," Brother Owen says.

"There must be some mistake. These are cattle cars," I say slowly, watching bits of dust and straw swirl up in the sunlight each time Brother Owen stacks a bag. "They're for animals, Papa."

"And for shabby Mormons who don't have much

money," Papa says. Sister Owen laughs as Brother Owen lifts her into the car and gently brushes her hair from her rosy face.

Papa reaches for me. "Come, Charlotte."

I give him a limp hand and let him haul me into the car, which is soon stuffed with people. Our clothes smell sour with old seawater and sweat.

The doors slide shut with a crash. My throat closes. For the first time since leaving Liverpool, I cry. Like a weepy cow, I stick my head out between wooden slats so no one will see me.

The train begins to move, then gathers speed. Faster. Faster. The ties of my bonnet loosen and flap hard in the Boston breeze.

"Oh!"

The wind snatches my bonnet straight off my head and sends it soaring.

I blink and swallow air.

How high will it fly? How far will it go? Perhaps my flying hat will beat me to the prairie's edge, where our journey begins.

I start to laugh. My bonnet has broken free from this car.

Soon I will, too.

· *Prairie* ·

Monday, July 7, 1856

❦

NEAR MUDDY CREEK, IOWA

"Where are we going, Charlotte?" asks Hyrum Evans, younger brother of Elizabeth the Musical.

He is tagging me out of camp, along with several other children.

"It's a secret," I say.

And it's a fine morning for sharing my secret, too. The company is slow getting started because Brother Bowen's axle is broken. Also, a cow has wandered off, which caused Papa to curse when he heard the news.

Papa's talent for cursing has grown in America, though he thinks I don't hear him mutter.

"Is it true you found buried treasure?" pipes up Mary Edmunds, little sister of Elizabeth the Fair.

"Real buried treasure?" echoes Jacob Butler, brother of Elizabeth the Jolly.

"You'll see."

The children trot along like eager ponies sniffing about for oats. I tried telling their older sisters about my discovery last night as we gathered dried buffalo dung—chips—for our evening fires, but they wanted to talk about the way they had just wandered throughout the entire camp, which spreads on forever. They were looking at boys, including John, who they think is handsome and wild. Elizabeth the Musical sighed every time she said the word *wild*.

The spot I mean to explore is just ahead.

"This way," I say, lifting my skirts and stepping through grass, enjoying how it feels against my legs.

We stop in front of a large mound of earth.

Mary's round face falls. "An *anthill*, Charlotte?"

"Yes," I say, "but it isn't just any anthill, Mistress Mary. It's almost as tall as you. Besides, look at this." I reach into the pocket of my pinafore and pull out a small glass bead. It sparkles deep blue.

Mary claps her hands.

"Where did you find it?" Jacob asks.

I point at the anthill. "On the top. Right by the hole."

"But how did it get there?" Hyrum asks.

The children crowd around me. I can't resist.

"Thieves," I say. "Thieves who rob rich people and

hide their jewels in anthills because nobody ever thinks to look there. Nobody except for us and the ants."

I've seen beads like these on the clothes of the Indians we trade with sometimes. Ants must find the ones that fall off and carry them to their hills. But thieves make a better story than industrious insects.

Hyrum whoops out loud.

"Let's find some jewels!" says Jacob.

"We should hurry, though," says Mary, glancing over her shoulder for robbers.

Poor Mary. She looks so nervous. Should I tell her I am just teasing?

That would spoil the fun. "Mary's right. Be quick about it," I say.

Hyrum and Jacob have long sticks now. Together they start hollering and stirring up the anthill. Big red ants stream in straight lines down the sides of the mound.

"Watch out!" Mary screeches. "They'll bite us!"

I ignore Mary because I see beads everywhere. Beads of all shapes and colors and sizes.

Mam would have loved these.

I drop straight to my hands and knees and pluck them up from the earth as though they are hard tiny fruits. Greedy as an English landlord, I stuff them into my pockets. I am ashamed to admit it, but I even grab beads I see Jacob and Mary and Hyrum reach for.

Blue. Red. Black. Yellow. I can make bracelets for the

three Elizabeths and me. Decorate a purse. Sew them on my wedding dress.

Blue. Red. Black. Yellow . . .

"OUCH! OUCH!"

I leap to my feet and swat myself. I twirl around so that my skirt flares. I shake out my hair. Hop on one foot. Hop on the other.

Ants are crawling up my legs and down my back.

"Look at Charlotte dance!"

It's John Bowen and Hyrum's big brother, Morgan, watching me with huge grins on their dusty faces. If I weren't so busy slapping myself, I'd slap them both.

"Dance, Charlotte, dance!" Morgan says.

John claps his hands in time to the tune of an imaginary fiddle.

Of all the people I wouldn't choose to see me with a garland of ants in my hair, it would be John.

"Go away!" I shout, brushing at an ant behind my right ear. "You should be helping your father repair that broken axle of yours."

"I already have. That handcart is as good as new. Thanks to me."

"*Ouch!*" Another bite.

John and Morgan keep grinning.

"We were sent to tell you to return to camp," says Morgan. "Captain Bunker wants to address us."

"Please don't tell about the ants." I try to sound as if I'm not begging.

John just laughs as he swings Mary onto his shoulders and then squats down so that Jacob can crawl up on his back. Both children are giggling.

"Now for a horse ride back to camp!" he says. Then he jiggles them up and down as he trots, while I drag along behind.

Elizabeth the Fair runs to meet us.

Mary slips down John's back and races toward her sister as John trots off with Jacob.

"Look what Charlotte and I discovered!"

Elizabeth the Fair leans forward so that her forehead gently touches Mary's forehead—like a kiss. They look like twin dolls, only one is big, the other small. Elizabeth the Fair smiles, picks up one of Mary's pigtails, and lets it drop, which makes Mary giggle. Then she examines the beads on her little sister's palm.

"Just see how they shine in the sun!" Mary demands.

"They're lovely. Especially the red ones." Elizabeth the Fair looks up at me with admiration. "I'm sorry I didn't come with you after all, Charlotte."

I am so pleased that I almost forget about the ant disaster.

"You can have my red beads, Lizzie," says Mary.

Elizabeth the Fair laughs. "Thank you, Mistress Mary."

She slips a slender arm around Mary's shoulder and leads her to their mam.

Mary doesn't even say goodbye to me now that she has her big sister's attention.

As we wait for Captain Edward Bunker to address our company of three hundred people, I glance around and think how different we all look now than we did the day we boarded the *S. Curling*.

We are leaner. Browner, except for Papa, who grows redder and redder beneath the fierce sun because of his red hair. Our hands and feet are covered with blisters, and everything else is coated with trail dust. It blankets our teeth and our tongues and the backs of our throats, so that some days we struggle to swallow.

Who would have thought there would be so much trail dust in America?

But we do not look unhappy. Except for Sister Rosa Jenkins, whose husband, George, died of inflammation of the lungs a week before we landed in Boston.

The Mormon elders in charge of us during our voyage across the ocean told us to stay above board as much as possible to prevent the spread of disease. But Brother Jenkins became ill anyway. He was full of fever, tormented by labored breathing. His skin was gray and the edges of his lips turned blue. I heard Sister Bowen tell Papa that when George Jenkins finally died, Rosa fell to her knees and opened her mouth to scream but no sounds came out. She looked like a fish snatched up from the water—wide eyed and silent.

Brother Jenkins was buried at sea after a storm so furious we feared we would sink. And now Rosa is wasting away like her husband before her, although it is not her body that is sick, but her heart.

Then there is Catherine Jones, with her scarred face full of secrets.

The leader of our group, the Yankee captain Edward Bunker, does not speak Welsh, so he often uses Brother Roberts to translate for us. Which makes Brother Roberts think he is practically the prophet and president of the church himself.

I study Captain Bunker while he speaks, trying to understand at least a few of his English words before Brother Roberts turns them into Welsh ones. This is good practice for me before I get to Utah.

Also, it takes my mind off the fact that the day is already growing sticky and warm.

Small and lean, Captain Bunker is not really handsome. But he has a face that makes you look twice. His bright eyes are set deep and close to each other. His hair, which sometimes falls across his high sunburned forehead, is dark. His cheekbones look like chiseled stone.

It's a hard face. A soldier's face. Except for his mouth, which is quite nice to stare at during long boring meetings.

He was a member of the Mormon Battalion, our Captain Bunker. I shiver and smile when I think of the second verse of the song about the wolves that we learned on the ship.

The groans of the dying were heard in our camp,
And the cold chilly frost, it was seen on our tent,
And the fear in our hearts can never be told
As we listened to the howling
of those lonesome roving wolves.

I have no doubt that Captain Bunker was very brave. With us he is kind and mild, though he does have a wicked temper when he needs one, especially each morning when he helps yoke the oxen that pull the company's supply wagon.

Oxen are such stupid creatures. Cows, too.

"And so," says Brother Roberts, "Captain Bunker and his counselors have decided that because so many of our handcarts need attention, we will not move forward today."

A groan goes up from the group. Captain Bunker lifts his hand to silence us before he speaks.

"Use the time to help one another first, then attend to your own affairs," Brother Roberts translates as Captain Bunker mops his brow with a rough handkerchief.

It's almost time for dinner now, and everyone in camp has heard the story of "Charlotte and the Ants."

Everyone thought the story was funny, too, except for Sister Roberts, who just rolled her eyes as if I'm some personal plague she must endure. "Do you ever see the other girls your age digging up anthills?"

I started to tell her what Elizabeth the Fair had said

when she saw Mary's beads—how she wished she'd gone with me—but Sister Bowen made me hush.

"Come now, Lititia," Sister Bowen said, "there's no need to be so hard on our Charlotte."

"I am trying to help her grow up, Margaret," Sister Roberts said. Then she snatched my arm and inspected it for bug bites until I snatched it back.

Ants. John and Morgan. Sister Roberts. I fume as I unstrap a bucket from the side of the handcart. Papa and I brought more buckets with us, but we had to leave most of our things behind in Iowa City, where those of us from the ship were separated into smaller companies and outfitted for the rest of our overland journey by Mormon agents who live and work for the church there.

Along with daily provisions and supplies for the company as a whole, Papa was allowed to carry seventeen pounds of personal belongings—not an ounce more—in our handcart, which is nearly four feet long and has two enormous wheels. It was made in a hurry of unseasoned hickory wood and is already cracking in the heat. I was allowed only fourteen pounds. The brethren weighed our things to make sure we did not exceed the limits, although I fooled them by wearing a few utensils and some bedding beneath my dress.

Papa shot up his eyebrows when he saw me looking so plump that morning, and I entertained him by turning around in circles and bumping into things. "This is my new waddle dance!"

Still, I could not hide everything we owned, which I realized, after our first day on the trail, was a blessing. Oh, my poor muscles cried as I pushed our cart from behind while Papa grunted and pulled.

I hated to give up our belongings, though, as Papa and I picked through them piece by piece before leaving. Deciding what to take and what to put in storage with the faint hope we might send to Iowa City for them one day. Extra dishes. Clothes. Tools. Parting with such ordinary things was like saying goodbye to pieces of our life, especially when I handed over all of Mam's quilts except for two.

We still have a blue one the color of flax. A sunny yellow one, too, which I hid between my legs.

Everybody else in the company left belongings behind. Brother Giles left his lovely harp. It still makes me sad to think of his face when he told the agents in Iowa to keep it for him.

But we do have one bucket. One cursed bucket. Which I am now taking down to the river to fill. Time to start dinner. Again.

The days seem much the same to me.

Some people think water has no fragrance. But that's because they're not paying attention.

Ocean water is sharp and salty, whereas river water is thick and muddy yet somehow fresh at the same time.

My bucket is full, but I linger to hang my hot feet

in the silvery water and listen to birds. Upstream, a distant woman loosens her hair and bathes alone. Catherine Jones.

Catherine Jones isn't the only woman making the trek to Zion without the help of a husband. There were a number on board the *S. Curling*—young women and spinsters and widows. There was even one woman, traveling with two daughters, who had left her husband behind in England because he wouldn't join the church.

In our own company we have the Widow Rogers and, of course, Rosa Jenkins, who share handcarts with families that were assigned to them by Captain Bunker at the beginning of our trek.

Catherine Jones pulls her cart alone.

I don't know how she manages. She is tall but slender, and some days her face is so red with effort that I think she will burst into flame and set the prairie on fire. Still, she toils on, stubborn and solitary.

Grass rustles behind me. I turn to see Sister Mary Owen coming for her own dinner water. She is even slower and larger and oddly more graceful than she was that day on the ship when we shouted goodbye to Wales together.

"Hello, Charlotte. Will you promise to help me up if I sit down by you?"

I laugh and nod. She eases herself to the ground, takes off her shoes, and dangles her feet in the water, too.

"It's pleasant by the river in spite of all the insects, isn't it?" says Sister Owen. "I feel less dusty just looking at it. And I love the way it smells."

I laugh. "Papa teases me about the way I always notice how things smell. He says I'm like a hound dog."

"Thomas teases me, too." Sister Owen smiles, then shakes her head. "Wait until you're carrying a baby, Charlotte. Your sense of smell grows even sharper."

Me? Carrying a baby? I cannot imagine it!

We sit together and enjoy the late-afternoon light for a moment. I'd love to live by Brother and Sister Owen and their new baby when we get to Utah. We could sit on a step and watch the sun linger at the end of a summer's day.

But I will probably never see the Owens again when our journey together is over.

I swallow a sigh, then show Sister Owen the beads from the anthill.

"What will you do with them?" she asks with a smile.

I shrug as I slip the beads back into my pocket. "Make myself a fancy purse someday, I suppose."

"A fancy purse would be very nice."

Soon the fireflies will appear and do their nighttime dance.

"Ouch! Stop it!" says Sister Owen suddenly. Then she laughs. "This naughty baby is kicking my poor ribs hard." She puts her hand on her stomach. "I can feel its foot right there." She shifts her hand. "And there's its tiny bum."

Sister Owen laughs and so do I.

"Here, Charlotte, feel for yourself."

I hesitate.

"Go ahead," she says. "I don't mind."

So I touch Sister Owen's swelling belly and feel the baby shift inside.

"Oh!" I squeak. "Did that hurt?"

She smiles and shakes her head. "Feeling the baby move is always a private pleasure for me. I will have to share this child with everyone else soon enough. But the pains hurt. They started up last night for a while, then stopped."

"Are you afraid, Sister Owen?" I ask.

Sister Owen looks at me with honest hazel eyes. "I won't lie to you, Charlotte. I *am* afraid. All the sisters say how fierce the pain is."

I remember the sounds Mam made and the way I used to hide so I wouldn't have to hear her.

"It must hurt a great deal," I say slowly.

Sister Owen plucks a tiny yellow flower and chews daintily on its stem. "I'm more worried about what I will do after the baby comes. I know the sisters will help me, but . . . but I miss my own mam. In spite of everything."

I nod.

Dear God, please bless and keep my mam, too.

And now it's night. I'm sitting on a log away from camp. Alone.

I've finished my chores for the day. Cooking. Washing up. Gathering more buffalo chips for fuel.

Elizabeth the Jolly still refuses to touch the chips with her bare hands. She shrieks and uses two sticks to pluck them out of the grass, which makes the rest of us want to laugh or slap her, depending upon our mood.

I glance back at camp and see our company's tents surrounded by a circle of handcarts. The tents are square and large. Thirteen people are assigned to our tent. The Bowens. Catherine Jones. The Robertses. Ellenor and Elias Lewis, who are newly married. Sister Rosa Jenkins. Her babies, Emma and George. Papa and I.

No one is coming for me. Not yet, anyway.

Good.

I take out the knife Papa gave me for my very own and play mumblety-peg by starlight.

The three Elizabeths don't own knives, and I'm sorry for them. Mumblety-peg is an excellent game to play when you are angry. You throw your knife hard and see how deep you can make your blade dig into the dusty ground.

I'm playing *very* well tonight as I remember the way John and Morgan teased me over dinner with their made-up ant songs.

I throw my knife. Pick it up. Throw it again. Over and over. I don't even take the time like I usually do to examine my blade between tosses and savor the way it gleams.

A rustle.

"Ah. Somehow I thought I'd find you here." Papa joins me, his hat in his hands. He is grinning. "I asked myself where my daughter would be listening to the stars sing tonight, and here she is. Throwing a knife."

"Hello, Papa." I give him a tragic sigh as I make my knife bite the ground again.

"I need my toes," says Papa. "Be careful."

"You're teasing me too," I say.

Papa is quiet, although he still smiles at me.

"Everybody believes I'm a baby," I say at last, wishing with all my heart that people thought better of me.

"Not a baby. A young girl. Who will be a woman like her mam one day."

He sits down by me and pulls me close. I can't help smiling. I put my head on his shoulder, and the dust from his shirt fills my nose.

"Your papa is so kind," Elizabeth the Musical once said to me.

Hers is serious and stern. He expects his children to obey him immediately, and if they don't, he makes free with his hand.

I look up at the stars and wonder if Mam is there tonight.

"I was proud of John today," Papa says, watching fireflies. "He repaired the handcart Rosa Jenkins travels with and made her laugh while he was doing it. It's been a while since we have heard our Rosa laugh."

Papa strokes his beard and gazes at the sky. "John has the makings of a fine carpenter, which I mean to tell his father. James is the best of men, but sometimes he is too hard on the boy."

"I hate John, Papa."

"You're . . . embarrassed right now, Charlotte. But that will pass. Good things. Bad things. Everything passes." He chuckles. "By morning you'll feel better and see for yourself how funny the story of 'Charlotte and the Ants' is. We all know how much Charlotte Edwards loves a good story. You'll be telling it to your own grandbabies one day."

Maybe.

But probably not.

Thursday, July 10, 1856

❧

OUTSIDE DES MOINES, IOWA

Something wakens me. I flip onto my back and listen.

Is it the wolves again? Their chorus of howls often awakes me here.

> *The grave of the stranger we left on the plain*
> *Down by the green grove, there forever to remain.*
> *To remember his grave we left ashes and coals*
> *To hide him from the savages and the lonesome*
>   *roving wolves.*

One day I'll tell my grandchildren that I used to see the devil creatures at the fringes of our camp each night. I'll tell them how their eyes gleamed green and how their sharp teeth glistened silver in the moonlight. I'll say that the wolves often plotted among themselves to eat us up, poor and scrawny and foul-tasting Welsh things though we were. . . .

The truth is I've never seen a wolf, although the animals do follow us at a distance.

Still, it would make a fine story—the kind that sends merry shivers down the back. It would make a much better tale, for example, than the story of "Charlotte and the Ants."

I hear a noise again. Something prowls just outside our tent's entrance.

An animal in search of food?

We have seen so many creatures since the day we left Iowa City, pulling our handcarts behind us. Prairie dogs with their funny little towns. Jackrabbits. Slinking coyotes. Wild white horses. Wave after wave of buffalo. Snakes.

Perhaps it's an Indian.

I think of the Indians we've traded with for food and other supplies. None of them has hurt us, but they are so very strange in their looks and in their clothes and in the way they feel free to reach out and touch your skin and your hair.

The flap moves. "Margaret?"

It's the Widow Rogers, who looks angry even when she is not. Most of her teeth are missing, which is part of the problem.

Sister Bowen, who sleeps at the far end of the tent

with her family, snores and rolls over. I love the fact that Sister Bowen thinks she doesn't snore.

"Margaret!" The name whistles through the gaps in the Widow Rogers's mouth.

"Who calls me?" asks Sister Bowen. She sounds groggy.

The Widow Rogers steps carefully into our tent and picks her way over a jumble of people until she reaches Sister Bowen.

"Young Mary Owen has had her baby but isn't well."

An icy finger touches my heart.

Sister Bowen sits straight up, wide awake. "Tell me."

"Our Mary started bleeding after delivering the child. We can't make her stop. But you—you have some skill as a nurse."

Sister Bowen leaps to her feet and follows the Widow Rogers out of the tent.

But wait.

A third woman steals after them.

I squint to make out who it is. Catherine Jones.

Catherine Jones?

I lie quiet and consider the Widow Rogers's words: *Our Mary started bleeding after delivering the child. . . .*

That's what I remember. The blood. Running down both sides of the bed.

Even though the night air is thick and warm, I pull Mam's yellow quilt up around my ears, curl into a ball, and think again of the babies.

I can tell you their names.

Ann. William. Owen. Robert. David.

I say the list to myself backward and forward when I cannot sleep so I will not forget them, even though they died as soon as they were born. It is my way of saying to God that those children would have mattered to us.

David. Robert. Owen. William. Ann.

David was the last, but it is Ann I think about the most. What would she look like? Dark and small and quick as a bird, like Mam? Or big and red haired, like Papa?

Maybe she would resemble me the way Mary looks like Elizabeth the Fair. My image in a mirror, only smaller. Brown hair. Brown eyes. Brown skin like acorns.

Maybe Ann would be like me in other ways, too. Maybe she would talk too much and laugh too loudly and tell untrue stories. Maybe she would be greedy and selfish sometimes and make people cross with her.

Or maybe she would be different. Elizabeth the Musical has a sister named Sarah who croaks like a frog when she sings evening hymns.

I am always watching the pairs of sisters in our company. The way they share food. Give each other sidelong glances when Sister Roberts lectures them. Burst into giggles over private jokes. Put their heads together when they wash up at night.

Oh, I would have loved my sister, Ann, no matter what she was like.

It was because of Ann and the other babies that Mam listened to the Mormons.

They came to the valley when it was green and full of lilacs. Sometimes when I close my eyes, I can still smell those lilacs, even though it's summer and the prairie air is so heavy with heat I feel as though I carry stones inside my chest.

Mam wanted nothing to do with the missionaries, even though the Bowens had joined the Mormon Church the spring before. Mam was angry with God for stealing her babies and sending them to hell before her priest could baptize them.

"Mormons don't baptize their babies, Barbara," Sister Bowen said one day as she and Mam worked side by side, doing the wash they took in to make extra money.

Mam looked at Sister Bowen with wonder and agreed to listen to the missionaries.

We met the Bowens and the missionaries in a bright green field on a bright Sunday afternoon. One was thin as a pole. The other looked like a mountain with a beard.

Mam did not smile when Sister Bowen made introductions. No. She was ready for a fight. Mam was always a fine fighter.

"I was told you Mormons don't baptize your babies. Is this true?"

The mountain with the beard nodded.

"Why not?"

"Why should we?"

"So they won't go to hell."

"Why would babies go to hell?"

"Because they have not been cleansed of sin."

Mountain smiled. So did Pole.

"God deliver us from sinful babies," said Pole.

"Gambling babies," said Mountain.

"Drinking babies."

"Cussing babies."

"Lying babies."

"Cheating babies."

"Thieving babies."

I laughed, and so did Papa and the Bowens.

Not Mam. "What if a baby dies before he is baptized?"

Mountain looked closely at Mam and grew serious. "When a baby dies, Sister Edwards, that little spirit is welcomed straight back into the outstretched arms of a loving God."

The spring air around us grew so silent, so still, the only thing I could hear was the names I sang in my head.

Robert. Owen. William. Ann.

I was afraid to see some fresh sadness in Mam's face, so I stared at her hands, balled into tiny hard fists.

"Now, how can that be true?" she whispered.

"Because that baby did not sin and was not tainted by

sin. Adam's sins were his own. We baptize our children when they are eight years old. They know the difference between right and wrong for themselves then."

Mam's hands unfolded slowly. She turned to Sister Bowen.

"Margaret, I think we would like to listen to the message these gentlemen bring."

Within the year we became Mormons. A year after that, our family and the Bowens decided to join the other saints in America. Best of all, Mam was expecting another baby. She took my hands and danced with me in the narrow street in front of our house when she told me the news, and I hoped with all my heart it would be another Ann.

But by Christmastime Mam was dead. So was the baby. Papa and I called him David, and we buried him in Mam's stiff arms.

Ann. William. Owen. Robert. David.

Tonight, in the dark tent, it is the blood that I remember.

Friday, July 11, 1856

❧

"Twenty years ago, Sister Mary Owen was born by the sea in Wales. Today we bury her in the belly of this great American prairie," says Brother Bowen.

I have always loved Brother Bowen's voice—deep and full of a wave's regular music. Even when his words are sad, the sound of them washes over you and gives sweet comfort.

We're clustered around Mary's grave. Her husband, Thomas, stands like a stone at its head. His arms are empty, and I wonder about that baby born in the dark hours of this morning. I haven't seen it yet. I don't even know whether it is a girl or a boy!

Thomas Owen is flanked by Captain Bunker, who holds his hat in his hands. His sunbaked face is grim.

Sweet Mary herself lies fresh in the earth, still uncovered by a blanket of dirt. She wears her good dress. Her fingers hold a snowy white handkerchief.

"It belonged to her mother," I heard Ellenor Lewis explain to the women who were laying Mary out. "It was the only thing of hers she had. The woman cut her off the day Mary walked into the waters of baptism to become a Mormon girl. Poor lamb." And then Ellenor began to weep.

I scan the crowd and find Ellenor. She is weeping still. Her husband, Elias, drapes an arm around her shoulder and pulls her close to him.

" 'To every thing there is a season, and a time to every purpose under the heaven . . . ,' " says Brother Bowen.

Mary wears a wreath of wild grapevines on her head. Her long loose hair, dark and shining in spite of death, reminds me so much of Mam I cannot breathe. Mam used to love it when Papa would comb out her hair at night. Papa, who stands next to me, reaches for my hand and holds it tight.

I know he's thinking of Mam, too.

" 'A time to be born, and a time to die . . .' "

Sister Bowen looks into the grave at Mary's still face. John listens closely to his father.

" 'A time to plant, and a time to pluck up that which is planted . . .' "

Rosa Jenkins holds Emma on her hip. She doesn't move when little George lifts her skirts up high and hides beneath them. She is thinking of another burial. One at sea.

" 'A time to kill, and a time to heal . . .' "

Brother and Sister Roberts huddle together.

" 'A time to break down, and a time to build up . . .' "

Catherine Jones stands, as always, a little apart from the others.

" 'A time to weep, and a time to laugh . . .' "

Brother Bowen pauses and looks at Thomas Owen, who stares straight ahead.

"Sister Owen, there will indeed be another time to laugh—on the great and glorious morning of that first Resurrection when we, your brothers and sisters in Christ, will join you with much shouting and laughing and glad clapping of hands. Until then, we will help the Lord care for your husband and your daughter."

Ah! The baby's a girl! Just like our Ann.

"So fear not, Mary. Although it is easy to forget, we will not forget. We will hold you dear and safe in our hearts always."

Papa squeezes my hand. I glance at his eyes and see tears there.

Brother Bowen finishes his speech. We sing.

"And should we die before our journey's through,
Happy day! All is well!

ask after her," Ellenor grumbles, rubbing her sore bare feet. She accidentally left her beloved pair of shoes on the banks of the Missouri River, so she is walking barefoot to Zion. "How can he ignore her when the baby is the very image of Mary?"

"Which is the reason he avoids the child," a low voice whispers behind me.

I practically shoot out of my stockings. I whirl around and find Catherine Jones, cloaked in shadows. "Eaves-dropping again, Charlotte?" she whispers to me before stepping into the light of the fire.

"Good evening, Catherine," says Sister Bowen. The others sitting around the campfire acknowledge her.

She returns their greeting with a graceful nod. Is it possible that Catherine Jones was once beautiful?

My heart turns over.

Will I be beautiful someday?

Will I go to bed one night, all knobby knees and sun-rough skin, and wake up a fine, smooth-skinned lady the next?

Will boys ever look at me the way they look at Elizabeth the Fair?

I have my doubts, frankly.

"I've just left Rosa Jenkins," Catherine Jones reports crisply to the group. "She wants me to tell you that she can't have full responsibility for the girl. Rosa will continue to nurse the baby as one of her own, since she is the only woman in our company who can do so at the moment. But the baby's primary care must go to someone else."

Sister Bowen sighs, shifts her weight, and stretches her plump legs out in front of her. She wriggles her sore toes. "It's been too easy for us to leave the baby with Sister Jenkins, who already has more than she can attend to."

I know it's wicked of me to feel this way about a widow with two small children, but I don't much care for Rosa Jenkins these days. She is so unkempt. Buttons always undone. Lank hair loose and grubby petticoats dragging through the dust.

When we share our testimonies on Sunday evenings, Sister Jenkins stands before us and weeps, saying how much she loves her children. Who am I to judge? But can she truly love George and Emma when she ignores them as she does?

I'll *never* ignore my children. They'll always be well cared for. And clean, too.

"Oh, I'd love to throttle Thomas Owen for not looking after his own!" Ellenor says.

Ellenor is one of those people who can say whatever they want to say without making people angry with them. I must learn this trick from her.

Sister Bowen flashes Ellenor a brief grin. "And so would I. But let's try not to judge him too harshly during his season of grief. I think I know what kind of a man Thomas Owen is. The day will come when his heart will claim his child."

"I hope you speak true, Margaret," says Sister Roberts. "Until then, we must make a plan for the child's care."

The sisters nod among themselves as the fire before them crackles.

"We can take turns tending the baby," Ellenor says.

"Yes," says Sister Bowen. "I could carry her one day, you another, Lititia another—"

"Poor thing," says Ellenor, "passed around camp like a basket of dirty laundry."

"At least the child lives," Sister Roberts points out. There is an edge to her voice that I do not understand.

Sometimes I wonder what she was like when she was my age. I'm sure I would have pulled her hair.

"True, Lititia," says Sister Bowen. "The child lives, and it's our duty to do right by Mary Owen's baby."

There are murmurs of agreement.

"Well, then," says Sister Roberts, "what about tomorrow?"

Mam used to say this to me: "Charlotte, my dearest girl, one day you must learn to think before you speak."

I step out of the shadows and stand before everyone with my shoulders squared. I'm sure I look impressive in spite of the fact that my dress is too small for me. "I will care for the baby tomorrow!"

I don't know what I expect from these women. Maybe their gratitude. Not their laughter. Even Sister Roberts, the old prune, is smiling at me.

"Welcome, Charlotte," says Sister Bowen. "We were wondering when you would stop stumbling around in the dark out there and join us."

"You—you knew I was here all along?" I stammer.

"You're exactly like me, Charlotte," Ellenor giggles. "Too noisy by half."

"Noisy or no, your offer is both kind and generous," says Sister Bowen.

"And so very easy to make, especially since you have no idea what you're offering, Charlotte," says Sister Roberts.

"Lititia speaks the truth," says Catherine Jones. "A baby isn't a china doll to be played with, only to be abandoned when you've grown bored or distracted by the sight of pretty glass beads, Charlotte."

A red flush crawls up my neck. Everyone is thinking about the ants. Everyone is thinking that I'm a child. Worse than a child. A baby.

"You're wrong about me," I say, wishing that my voice would not shake so. I must learn the trick of speaking without showing emotion. You have power when you can do that.

Sister Bowen stands and slips her arm around my shoulders. "Come, Charlotte. Don't take offense when none was meant."

I'm so angry that I hear my heart pounding in my ears. I shrug Sister Bowen's warm arm from my shoulders and step a little away from her.

"I'll care for the child tomorrow," I say in my childish

shaking voice. "And the day after that. And the day after that," I shout at them. "I *will* carry that baby to Zion. Just see if I don't!"

Well! I've done it! I've left them all quite speechless.

Sister Bowen slowly plants her hands on her wide hips. She tilts her head to one side and looks me over. Then she turns to the others.

"What do you think of our Charlotte's offer here?" Sister Bowen asks.

I hope I'm not asked to speak, because my voice has turned to dust.

Will they laugh at me again? Tell me that I am a noisy child again?

A log pops and embers spray. Stars swirl over our heads, and beyond the swirling stars I imagine God himself watching.

I am going to faint.

"Hurrah for Charlotte!" Ellenor whoops. She leaps from her seat and hugs me. And then the rest of the women are thronging around me, full of advice.

"My husband and I will pray for you every morning and every night, Charlotte," says Sister Roberts.

I can tell she thinks I will need it.

Only Catherine Jones says nothing. She folds her arms across her bosom and watches me.

"What's all this commotion about?" Brother Bowen appears with a load of firewood on his back. John Bowen and Papa follow him.

"Daniel Edwards," says Sister Bowen, "your daughter has volunteered to take care of Thomas Owen's child until he can care for her himself."

Papa's eyes, full of wonder, find me. "Is this true?"

I nod.

"You'll be a fine woman one day," says Brother Bowen, smiling.

"Yes," says Papa. "Like your mam."

There is another pair of eyes upon me. I feel them on the back of my neck. I turn slowly and see John.

Watching me through the haze of gold and orange flames.

Monday, July 14, 1856

❧

MORNING

I didn't sleep well. No howling wolves this time. Only the knowledge that I've undertaken something enormous.

Oh, I was thrilled with myself last night. Especially after the women surrounded me and Papa looked at me with such pride. I was as grand as Queen Victoria on coronation day.

Then I went to bed and began making up stories about me and the baby to tell my children someday. How I saved the baby from wolves and Indians. How I rescued her when the Platte River flooded and destroyed Nebraska. How I protected her from more plagues than Moses ever dreamed of conjuring up to torture those Egyptians.

"Wasn't I brave?" I planned to ask my grandchildren. "Wasn't I noble?"

Then something horrible happened. I started to think.

I hate it when I think.

So now I am waiting outside our tent for Sister Jenkins to finish nursing this new baby who is only three days old and who cannot sit or stand or feed herself or tell me what I am doing wrong.

I could die.

Sister Bowen lifts the tent flap and emerges with a bundle in her arms. "The baby is clean and fed and ready to begin the day's journey."

I take a closer look at this bundle and find milky blue eyes staring straight up at me. The baby's skin is red and rough. Wrinkled. "She looks likes the Widow Rogers."

Sister Bowen laughs.

"And what happened to her head?" I squeak. "It isn't round, Sister Bowen. It's long and bumpy. Like a big potato."

A big potato covered with black hair.

The baby girl turns her head at the sound of my voice and tries to look at me in a wobbly sort of way.

"Oh, just look at how alert she is, Charlotte. Three days old and already responding to the sound of your voice," says Sister Bowen.

"Her head," I say again. "What happened to it?"

Sister Bowen laughs. "She was born, Charlotte. That's what happened to her head. Her head is fine. Trust me. A few more days and it will be as round as a full moon."

The baby opens her mouth, burps, and stretches out her neck. Then she snuggles back into her blanket and makes little mewing noises. Just like a kitten.

"Here now, Charlotte," says Sister Bowen. "Here's how you hold a baby. Like this. See how I have her neck?"

I am tasting fear.

"And watch this spot on the top of her head. It is very soft and must be protected."

I stare at the pulsing spot on the top of the baby's head.

"Your turn now," says Sister Bowen.

"Already?"

Sister Bowen nods.

I hesitate, to see if God has another plan for me— such as making the prairie open its mouth like Jonah's whale and swallow me whole.

Nothing happens.

I take a deep breath. Spread my feet. Close my eyes. Shoot out my arms.

Sister Bowen snorts with laughter. "Oh, Charlotte!"

I open one eye.

"This poor baby will roll right out of arms like those. Here, girl. Bend those elbows. And open your other eye."

"What if I drop her?" I open my other eye but do not bend my arms.

Sister Bowen smiles. "I wouldn't drop her to find out, if I were you."

"But what if I do?"

"Stop it, Charlotte. You'll be fine." Sister Bowen sounds so sure that I finally bend my elbows a little.

There. My arms look more like a cradle now.

"That's better, I suppose," says Sister Bowen. "Don't be afraid of her. Babies are much sturdier than they look."

She shifts the bundle from her arms into mine.

"Oh!" I cry, surprised by the delicious warmth of this little girl baby in her blanket. I pull her closer, so that her head is right against my cheek. Without thinking, I kiss her feathery black hair.

"Do all baby heads smell this good?" I ask.

"Yes. But the newborn scent doesn't last long, so enjoy it."

I kiss her head again. Then again. I cannot get enough of this strange baby perfume.

When I look up, I am startled to see that Sister Bowen's cheeks are moist. If this were Ellenor standing in front of me with a sopping face, I wouldn't be surprised. But Sister Bowen is like me. Stingy with tears.

I am alarmed. "What's the matter?"

Sister Bowen is her old self when she finally answers. "Lordy, I am becoming as fanciful as my husband. I just saw Barbara in you."

Mam.

I try to listen as Sister Bowen gives me more instructions on how to care for this girl baby, but her words sing through my head.

I just saw Barbara in you.

"So there you are," says Sister Bowen. "Shield her head at all times or it will burn in the sun like Brother Bowen's bald spot. Take her to Sister Jenkins when she gets hungry."

Panic rises in my throat. "How will I know she's hungry?"

Sister Bowen laughs. "Trust me. You'll know."

"And what should I call her?"

"Brother Owen hasn't given her a name yet. I'll leave that up to you and your papa." Sister Bowen touches the tip of the baby's nose and smiles at her. "When we break camp this morning, I'll strap her to your back. That way you can still help push the handcart."

"I have one more question."

"Another question? How very unlike you, Charlotte."

I ignore this little joke. "Why doesn't Catherine Jones like me?"

Sister Bowen snorts. "Don't be silly. Catherine doesn't dislike you."

"Why did she give me such cold looks last night,

then? She never looks at the other girls the way she looks at me."

I know that I'm a difficult person to like sometimes, even though I don't mean to be. Still. She could have at least smiled at me.

"The fact that Catherine notices you at all tells me she does not dislike you. She's a good woman in her own way. Catherine was a steady help to me the night Mary delivered this baby. She knows more than I do about herbs and their uses."

"Because she's a witch," I mutter.

The baby in my arms whimpers, then falls silent. My shoulders stiffen.

"What did I do wrong? Why did she just make that noise?"

Sister Bowen laughs. "She cried because that is what babies do, Charlotte. They cry. As you'll soon discover."

Sister Bowen cocks her head and looks me over. "You'll also discover how heavy she is for such a small load."

"Well, I'm very strong."

Sister Bowen takes my chin in her right hand and searches my face. "You'll have to be."

"Dust storm!" someone cries.

Sister Bowen turns away from me and this baby with no name. She shields her eyes and squints into the morning sun.

"It'll be upon us before we know it," she says.

Not far from camp, dust kicks up like great dirty waves in an angry ocean. Cows bellow, horses whinny, chickens squawk. Everyone scrambles to gather up things that might blow away.

"What do I do with this baby?" I shout at Sister Bowen, hoping she'll take her back.

"Use your head, girl!" Sister Bowen shouts back as she begins snatching up laundry. "Cover her face and hold on to her!"

A young mother from one of the other tents calls for her children. A small boy and an even smaller girl race toward her.

"Here!" The mother lifts her skirts. "Quick!"

The children dart beneath her dress, which she drops like a curtain over them.

I fumble for a corner of the blanket, pull it over the baby's face, and hold her against my chest as I crouch down, bending over her.

A spray of dust stings my eyes and shoots up my nose before I can duck my head. I swallow dry earth swirling in air and feel prairie grit raining against my cheek. Through my eyelashes I see the wind make campfires leap sideways. Tent flaps wave like the sails of a ship. Pans strapped to the sides of handcarts clatter. The back end of one of the tents collapses. It looks like an ox lowering itself to the ground.

I can see the outlines of the boy and girl moving beneath their mother's skirt.

And then it's over. For a fraction of a moment, the camp is as still as a graveyard. Then it stirs to life.

I spit out dust that has collected in my mouth. My heart pounds. Did the baby survive?

Slowly, I lift the flap from her face.

She blinks hard in the day's dusty light.

Monday, July 14, 1856

❧

EVENING

Oh, my poor back. My shoulders, too, especially where the baby's sling I made from a shawl bit into my skin all day long.

We've stopped for the day, and I have stolen away by myself to the river's edge to soak my feet in its cool water while Sister Jenkins nurses the baby. Again.

I had no idea such a small person could eat so much in one day.

This is what the baby did today as I carried her on my back.

She slept.

She made little messes, which Sister Bowen showed me how to clean up. She cried. She ate.

This isn't a lot of activity. After all, the baby isn't George Jenkins, scampering around his mother's feet like a wild rabbit. She isn't Emma Jenkins, who rides high on Sister Jenkins's back.

And yet I'm exhausted. I lift my feet out of the water, then flop down on a bed of cool river grass and stretch out all my numb limbs and hope I never *ever* have to get back up.

It wasn't so terrible at first. The three Elizabeths crowded around and fussed over the baby. They acted as if they envied me. Everyone else in the company commented on what a fine thing it is that I'm doing, and their praises rang like music in my ears.

But by the time the hot sun was sitting in its noonday seat, it seemed that people had already grown used to the sight of Charlotte Edwards hauling a brand-new baby around on her back.

Then when the axle on Brother Bowen's handcart broke and one of the Widow Rogers's chickens got loose, I was forgotten.

Well, not quite.

Papa, of course, offered to carry the baby, which was silly because he pulls most of the weight of the handcart. Sister Bowen, too, was always close at hand, and even Sister Roberts asked if she could help.

Then there was John.

He never said anything to me about the baby. But I caught him looking at me.

As Papa and I bowed our heads to pray over our supper, I said a secret prayer.

Dear God, I think I might only have been teasing last night when I said I wanted to carry the baby to Zion. Please make Thomas Owen want his daughter back soon. . . .

"Charlotte?"

I turn and see Papa smiling. He's returned from Rosa Jenkins with the baby in his arms.

"She finished her dinner and fell asleep," Papa says. "May we join you?"

"Please do." I sit up. "But mind the insects. They fly into my mouth whenever I speak. Maybe it's a sign from God that I should give up talking."

Papa laughs. I love the fact that he thinks I'm funny even when no one else does.

"Life would be very dreary for me if you ever stopped talking, Charlotte," he says as he sits down beside me, taking care not to wake the baby.

I peek at her and smile.

"She's charming when she's asleep," I point out.

Papa winks at me. "Most children are."

We watch for the evening's first fireflies together. Soon there will be prayers and songs and perhaps ghost stories.

"Was I ever that small?" I ask Papa.

"Smaller," he says, "though I can hardly believe it now."

The baby wriggles. Did we wake her? No. She nestles against Papa's broad chest and he grins.

Now, here's an interesting thing. Although she sleeps, the baby holds her tiny hands in front of her like pink fans.

"Do all babies do that?"

"You did. For a while. And then it passed." Papa takes one of her hands and kisses her fingers. One by one by one. "Mam and I used to kiss your fingers just like that."

I watch her to see what tricks she'll do next.

"It is funny how much pleasure there is in watching a baby sleep," Papa says. "We used to watch you sleep, Charlotte."

The old fear stirs my heart. Papa remembers so much about Mam. So does Sister Bowen.

Then why is Mam slipping away from me?

"I've been thinking," Papa says. "We should give this little girl a name she can use until her father claims her."

"When do you think that will be?"

Papa shrugs. "It could be in a few days. . . ."

I feel a quick flutter of hope.

"Or it could be after our journey is over."

I sigh.

Cradling the baby with one arm, Papa slips the other one around my shoulders. A river breeze lifts my hair.

"Either way, you must prepare for the day when it happens."

Prepare? I'm ready to hand Brother Owen his daughter this very minute. I nod. Then I look again at the bundle in Papa's arms.

Well, she *is* beautiful, even if her skin is flaky and her

head looks like a bumpy potato. She isn't quite so red tonight. She's pink. Like a rose.

"Let's not give her an ordinary name, Papa," I say. "Not Elizabeth. Do we really need any more of them?"

Papa laughs. "What should we call her, then?"

I remember that scrap of Scripture. *And the desert shall rejoice, and blossom as the rose!*

Mam loved roses. I remember that much.

"Rose," I say. "Her name is Rose."

And then I reach for my Rose baby, and for the first time I say aloud the words I have been stitching together in my head today.

> *"We're going to a new place,*
> *a safe place,*
> *a place for us to play*
> *and a place for us to grow,*
> *a place where girls will tend their houses*
> *and their gardens dressed with roses!"*

Rose opens her eyes and I laugh, and I know that each night she is with me—for however long that is—I will sing this poem to her beneath a bright spill of stars.

"Wake up, Sister Jenkins," I whisper. "Please."

Rosa Jenkins doesn't answer, doesn't move.

I hate to disturb her dreams again because she looks happy. Or peaceful, at least. Beautiful, too, with her hair fanning out from her head like glossy wings. She looks the way she did when I first saw her on the ship.

The tent is filled with night noises—breathing, tossing and turning, moaning, Papa talking in his sleep, Sister Bowen snoring, Rose whimpering at Papa's side.

Am I the only person who hears her?

I glare at Papa across the sea of sleeping bodies that separates us. His arm is flung over his head as if he hasn't a care in the world. Can't he hear her? He should. He's heard her all the other times tonight. Why doesn't he wake up and help me again?

"Sister Jenkins!" I give her a little shake this time.

She blinks. "What is it?"

"Rose is hungry."

"I just nursed her."

"But that was over a half an hour ago."

"She isn't hungry, Charlotte. Now, let me sleep before I have to feed my Emma." Sister Jenkins turns away.

What should I do?

Rose bleats. I make my way back over to my family's corner. Then I pick her up and pack her outside into the night's heat.

It's hard to sleep when it's warm and muggy. Especially if you have a baby girl by your side whom you worry about rolling on top of and squashing like a bug while you sleep. If you could sleep, that is, which you can't because that baby keeps wailing in your cursed ear.

Wales never gets this hot. I close my eyes, remembering

the narrow streets of Port Talbot. How it felt to run down them, laughing hard, as cool Welsh air touched my skin.

I would go back there tonight if I could. I think Rose's mother would, too, if she were still alive.

I pace in front of the tent, jostling Rose in my arms, which are full of cramps because I'm so tired.

How am I supposed to walk twenty miles tomorrow if I don't sleep twenty minutes tonight? You would think God could have arranged things a little better when he created babies.

I throw back my weary head. Look at the sky. Find the Plow. Draw a line and extend it. Say hello to the North Star.

"I don't want to do this," I tell my friend Polaris. Then I stick my head through the tent door and look down on Papa, who guards the entrance like a red bear even when he sleeps.

"Papa!"

He ignores me.

"Wake up!"

He snorts.

"Fire!"

Papa shoots straight up, his hair and eyes wild.

"I need you, Papa. Now."

Papa stumbles outside, glances around, then gives me the glum stare of a dog who knows you can and you will take his bone away from him.

"That was a wicked trick, Charlotte."

"Well, it was very wicked of you to abandon me."

Papa's jaw drops. "I've been up with you and Rose all night!"

It's true. He has. I start to feel guilty for waking him, which makes me even crosser. "Brother Owen should take care of his own baby."

The injustice of it!

Papa snorts and stomps around, searching for the words he wants to say. He finally snaps at me in a loud voice, "You asked for this responsibility, Daughter. No one forced you to do it. Why did you volunteer? Were you just showing off for the sisters?"

Tears spring to my eyes. Oh, how can Papa—*Papa*—be so cruel?

Neither of us says anything. Then Papa smooths down his wild hair and sighs. "Give her to me, Spooky Sue," he says, calling me an old nickname he hasn't used for years. "I'll watch her while you sleep."

Quiet tears of frustration slip down my cheeks.

"I miss Mam," I say.

"I know. So do I."

I slide Rose into Papa's arms.

"We'll muddle through somehow, Charlotte."

Muddle through? I know Papa means to comfort me. But he doesn't need to, because as of this very moment I have devised a plan.

Tuesday, July 15, 1856

"You're so right, Sister Charlotte. A father should care for his own. Meanwhile, thank you for tending my daughter last night. No one could have done a finer job. But I'm feeling much better, as you can see for yourself, and I want my baby back."

I nod graciously at Brother Owen as he sweeps his hat off his head and kisses my cheek.

Then I hand over Rose.

This is the conversation I have in mind when I approach Thomas Owen, who's eating breakfast just ahead with the people from his tent. Surely he won't turn me and his own daughter away in front of them.

But I'm losing heart with each step I take in his direction.

What if he says no?

He might. He gave her up, after all. Will he really want her back?

And what will the others think of me if I force Thomas Owen to do his duty as a father, especially after all the noise I made about taking this baby in the first place?

My feet drag. They're as heavy as my arms, which are loaded down with Rose.

I stop some yards away. Perhaps I'll attract Thomas Owen's attention by standing here on the fringes of his group. That way he can leave the others and speak with me in private.

Rose, who has her nights and days mixed up, is sleeping soundly. This is excellent because she's attractive when she sleeps. Brother Owen may want her back if he sees her like this, snuggled against my chest.

I wait to be noticed.

And wait and wait.

Everyone keeps eating.

Thomas Owen lifts his cup and looks past the group. Our eyes meet. His cup freezes in midair.

Come get your daughter, I say to him in my head.

Thomas Owen just stares at me. Then he presses his cup to his lips, takes a long sip, and turns away.

You and the child are invisible to me, he says without using words.

I am shaking as I wander, looking for Papa.

"Whoa!" says Elizabeth the Musical as I plow straight into her. "Charlotte, watch out."

She and her sister Sarah are headed for the river to wash up after breakfast.

"I'm sorry," I say, "but I can't see straight. This baby kept me up all night long."

"You sound so grumpy," says Sarah. Then she puts her face in Rose's face and makes silly kissing noises. "How could Charlotte be grumpy with a sweet girl like you?"

Rose mews, and I want to slap Sarah for waking her up.

"Can we take her for a while, Charlotte?" asks Elizabeth the Musical.

"It would be so much fun to play with her!" Sarah chimes in.

"Please, Charlotte," they say. "Please."

I give them both a grim smile as I slip the baby into Elizabeth's eager arms. Straightaway, she lets Rose's head flop.

"Mind her neck!" I snap as they carry her off.

I see her just ahead, walking in a huge bright skirt that billows across the prairie like the sail of a ship.

Mam.

I run after her, long grasses tickling my brown bare legs.

"Mam! Mam! It's me. Charlotte. Don't leave. Look at me. Please, Mam."

She stops. Sees me. Smiles. Spreads wide her arms.

I keep running toward her, happy to see her. Afraid she'll be gone before I can reach her.

Suddenly the wind lifts up Mam's skirt, filling the entire sky with it, and I see the children that have been hiding all along beneath her dress. Thousands of them, gathering around her ankles and holding on to her long legs, strong as slender trees.

I do not know who these children are. Just that they seek her sheltering skirt in a new country as the hot prairie sun streams down upon their dark Welsh hair.

"Charlotte?" It's Papa. Holding Rose. Looking gently down on me as I lie here in the shade of our handcart, blinking. I have a dim memory of stumbling here after Brother Owen ignored me, then dropping to the ground for a quick morning nap.

"I've let you sleep as long as I can, but now it's time to go."

I blink some more, then give Papa a weak grin.

"Well. I see that Elizabeth and Sarah have returned Rose."

He laughs. "They enjoyed playing house until their real baby wet herself. I can promise you they brought her back in a hurry after that."

"Who cleaned her?"

"Your old papa, of course. I told you we'd muddle through somehow."

I stand. Let Papa help me put Rose in her sling. Shake myself free of dust and dreams.

Thursday, July 31, 1856

❧

West of Florence, Nebraska

"But you just ate, Rose. How can you be hungry again!"

I push the handcart while Papa pulls, and I am dead sick of this baby crying on my back.

"Did you burp her after Sister Jenkins fed her, Charlotte?" Papa asks. "Perhaps she has air bubbles in her stomach."

"Of course I burped her."

Or at least I tried to. I slung Rose over my shoulder and patted her back forever. But she never burped. Burping a baby is a tedious job. I would rather gather buffalo chips. At least that way you're moving around.

Papa shifts our handcart to the side and stops.

Catherine Jones looks at the three of us as she passes us by, pulling her own cart.

"Bring Rose to me, Charlotte," Papa says.

I walk to the front of the handcart. Papa takes Rose from the sling and lifts her to his shoulder. Then he rubs her back. Rose belches like a toad and stops fussing immediately.

"Truly, you are magic, Papa!"

Rose turns her head at the sound of my voice.

"Sometimes rubbing a baby's back is better than patting it," Papa says. "And then sometimes patting a baby's back is better than rubbing it. Babies are fickle."

I laugh as he slips the baby back into her sling.

What new tricks will Papa surprise me and Rose with next?

Company members endure heat and ants. And of course there is the dust. We also contend with frogs, lice, boils, hail, locusts, and other Bible plagues.

(I am lying about the plagues. But the heat and dust are miserable. So are the ants!)

I continue to care for Rose, sometimes with an Elizabeth at my side, although I am currently very annoyed with Elizabeth the Musical. I was just explaining how hard it is to keep a baby's bottom clean and dry when she stopped dead in her tracks and planted her hands on her hips.

"Charlotte Edwards, you are always complaining about that baby! Stop it!"

I stomped away and did not speak to her for the rest of the day.

Meanwhile, Thomas Owen keeps his distance.

John keeps his distance, too.

Which is worse? John plaguing me or John ignoring me?

Here's another secret I haven't told a soul: I wish that John and I were friends as we used to be when we were young. The three Elizabeths are very nice. We like to talk and giggle and braid one another's hair, and sometimes we even examine anthills. Carefully. So far we have not discovered more beads.

But the Elizabeths are not John.

I turned thirteen yesterday, which means I am no longer a child. Sister Bowen shared her sugar with me to celebrate, which touched my heart because she is running low on supplies, like the rest of us. Also, I pulled my beads out and dreamed about the purse I will make myself from them when we arrive in Salt Lake. Right now I fancy the yellow beads, whereas last week I could not stop looking at the blue ones.

It was an ordinary day otherwise. We walked. We sang. We said night and morning prayers and listened to Scripture. Rose slept. Rose ate. Rose cried. Rose made more messes, which I did not tell Elizabeth the Musical about.

Later, Papa and Rose and I sat on a rock beneath the stars, where I sniffed the prairie air. It smelled of grass and earth and the skins of far-off animals.

Papa told me the story about the evening I was born. He tells me the same story every year, and I always enjoy it, even though I already know how it ends.

Last year Mam was with us when he told it. I wish I had known it was the last time then, because I would have memorized everything about her that day as though it were Holy Scripture.

After Papa told me the story, I looked at Rose in my arms and felt sad for her. The story about the day she was born is not a happy one. Her own father may not wish to tell it to her.

And she will not wish to hear it.

I asked Papa to hold Rose while I gathered a fistful of grass and wove a garland, which I placed like a crown upon Rose's dark head. Sister Bowen was right. Rose's head is round now. And her skin grows softer, too, like the back of a petal.

I sang the song I made just for her and ended it the way I always do.

A place where girls will tend their houses
and their gardens dressed with roses!

That was last night.
Tonight Brother Bowen has promised to tell ghost

stories to the people in our tent and the two tents that flank us.

"Now, this is a true story," Brother Bowen says.

His voice is a low purr. His white hair gleams whiter in the flickering light, and his smile is sly. The three Elizabeths and I sit huddled together near the campfire. Elizabeth the Musical braids Elizabeth the Jolly's hair. I listen to Rose's soft, fast breath and stroke her skin as she falls asleep in my arms.

"I know it's true," Brother Bowen says, "because it was told by a gentleman who traded with a man I knew back in Wales.

"This gentleman was traveling with his wife by carriage at night when they saw a young woman standing by herself in the center of a lonely crossroads. The evening was bitter cold, and the girl wore no cloak.

"'Please make the carriage stop,'" the gentleman's tenderhearted wife begged him. 'I do believe this young woman sorely needs our help!'

"So the wealthy man gave the order to stop his carriage, and he invited the young woman to join him and his wife.

"When she crawled inside the carriage, the man could see that this young woman was very beautiful, in spite of her dress, which was no longer fashionable, and her skin, which was paler than a winter's night.

"He could also see that she was greatly distressed.

" 'Have you seen him?' were her first words. Not 'Hello.' Not 'Please' or 'Thank you.' But 'Have you seen him?'

" 'Seen whom?' asked the wife with a quick glance at her husband.

" 'My Johnny with the laughing eyes,' said the girl. 'My parents have forbidden me to marry him, but they cannot stop me from eloping!'

"The girl gave a strange, desperate laugh, and the air inside the coach turned so cold, the man shivered. He and his wife looked at each other.

" 'We haven't seen your Johnny,' said the man gently.

"The girl's flimsy shawl slipped farther down her shoulder. 'But he was to come for me at noon!'

" 'I'm sorry,' said the wife.

"The girl began to weep and would not be comforted. 'He loves me,' she said over and over as the carriage wheels went round and round. 'I am certain he loves me more and more. I am certain he loves me and none other!'

"When the carriage came upon the next village, the girl stopped crying and looked out the window.

" 'Why, this is perfect!' she said, her pale face shining. 'I am certain my Johnny with the laughing eyes is waiting for me here now! Please stop at the inn ahead, for I know the place well. Thank you so much for your trouble.'

"This request made the man and his wife uneasy. But who were they to argue with a girl who so clearly knew her own mind? They left the young woman at the inn. She refused their generous offer of money.

" 'Oh, my Johnny will take care of me,' she said with a silver smile. Then she waved and disappeared into the inn.

"The gentleman and his wife continued on, but their unease grew until the man ordered the driver to return to the inn.

"He went inside to inquire about the strange, beautiful girl he had just left there. As he told his story, the innkeeper and his wife traded mysterious looks. Suddenly, the gentleman knew something was terribly wrong. He felt sure the innkeeper and his wife had done something to harm the poor young woman. No doubt, they had taken advantage of her youth and her confusion.

" 'What's going on here!' he said. 'Give me an answer immediately or you'll be sorry.'

" 'The girl you seek was called Sarah Lloyd,' said the innkeeper. 'She died this very night twenty years ago. Her fiancé never came, and she took her life here at the inn. She was buried as a suicide at the crossroads north of the village.'

"And that, Brothers and Sisters, is the true story of Johnny with the Laughing Eyes."

Firelight skips across Catherine Jones's face. The welt on her cheek is red and her eyes are empty. Elizabeth the Musical stops braiding Elizabeth the Jolly's hair. Several children squint their eyes shut or clap their hands over their ears. I look down at Rose snuggled in my arms.

Will she be afraid of ghost stories, too? Or beg for more, like me?

Could ghosts be real? I've never seen one. Still, the world is wide and bursting with mysteries that no one can explain. So why not ghosts?

Someone stalks out of the shadows, and I squeak.

It's no ghost, but Captain Bunker.

"You scared me!" I tell him, although he does not understand me. Instead, he just cocks an eyebrow at me, then nods a greeting at the rest of the group.

"Dancing tonight?" He attempts to say the words in Welsh. He mangles them, but I appreciate his effort.

Brother Bowen smiles at the captain. A cheer of agreement goes up, and our little group joins the rest of the camp. One of the brothers produces a fiddle, and all of us together dance like a vast ocean beneath a white rising moon.

Papa holds Rose and watches me dance.

At first she was fine. But now she is crying, crying, crying. Actually, that baby is raging like a storm at sea. Although I cannot see her tiny face, I know it must be bloodred by now and that she is pulling her legs up against her chest every time she screams. How can such a small creature make so much noise?

Dear God, please make Rose be quiet.

Rose sets up an unholy squall and I sigh.

"I've enjoyed dancing with you, Hyrum," I say, "but I must take care of Rose now."

Hyrum sweeps me a bow and trots off, looking for Elizabeth the Fair. They all trot off looking for Elizabeth the Fair, who's growing a chest. I noticed the other day as we bathed and splashed one another in the river. Elizabeth the Jolly teased Elizabeth the Fair until she blushed, then teased Elizabeth the Musical for being as flat as a boy.

I turned away in the water so that the three of them would not see what's happening to me.

I join Papa and peek at Rose. Frantic, she roots at Papa's shirt, looking for something to eat there.

"Sorry, little one," Papa laughs. "I don't have what you want."

"I'll take her to Sister Jenkins," I say.

Rose stops crying for a minute as Papa rolls her gently into my arms. My heart lifts a little. Could it be she likes me? Enough to stop crying?

Rose gazes thoughtfully at me with opaque eyes. Then she screws up her face and lets loose a howl that makes the prairie tremble.

Rosa Jenkins lies in our tent beside her sleeping babies, Emma and George. Her pale hair spills over her shoulders, and for a minute she reminds me of that girl in Brother Bowen's story.

"Rose is hungry," I say.

"Rose is always hungry. Everyone is always hungry. Everyone wants me to feed them." Sister Jenkins stares at the tent wall.

Rose screams and squirms in my arms. Sweat turns into beads on my forehead. What should I do? Feed her myself? Ha!

Little George stirs, although he doesn't wake. Sister Jenkins sits up and makes a move to touch his hair. Then she drops her hand, too tired.

Instead she bares a white breast and reaches up with thin arms. "Here, Charlotte. Give me the baby before she wakes up George."

So I hand over Rose, who latches on to Sister Jenkins and fills the tent with suckling sounds.

I've watched Sister Jenkins nurse Rose many times now. But I am still amazed at the way it all happens. It is a miracle, really. The baby just knows how to open her mouth and turn her head and find the milk she needs there.

Sister Jenkins looks up and smiles weakly. I remember how bright with sea air and hope she was when I first saw her on the ship.

"Why, look at you, Charlotte. You were just a little girl when we met. Now you're practically a woman."

Me?

"Leave Rose with me for a while. Dance tonight," says Sister Jenkins. "Dance while there is still time."

Fiddling fills the air as I join the group and clap in time. The three Elizabeths dance, their braids leaping out behind them. Some of the little children are giggling and jumping up and down. Elias spins Ellenor around and around. Brother Bowen slaps his thigh while Sister Bowen does a jig. A jig? Oh, she will be embarrassed for herself in the morning, I think. I search for Papa and find him speaking with Catherine Jones, who will not look at his face.

"Charlotte," says a familiar voice.

I stop clapping and turn. "Oh. It's you."

John frowns and jams his fists in his pockets. "Are you disappointed?"

I squint at him. "You are certainly very strange tonight, John."

He paces in front of me. To and fro. To and fro.

"Stop it," I tell him. "You're making me seasick."

He stops and coughs.

"Go away. I want to listen to the music." I nod at Elizabeth the Fair. "Why don't you go torment her, like all the other boys?"

John clears his throat. "Will you dance with me?"

Oh. I see how it is. He will start to dance with me, then step on my skirts or show me a snake he has hidden up my sleeve so I'll scream.

"No."

John's mouth pops open.

"You want to make me look foolish," I say.

He snorts then grabs my hands and pulls me into the circle so hard I practically collide with Ellenor Lewis, who dances like a dream with or without her shoes on. She grins and winks at us.

So. John and I dance. And dance. And dance across the prairie floor.

My skirt flares. My hair tumbles around my shoulders and face. The music rushes through my arms and my legs, my fingers and my toes.

I throw back my head and I start to laugh, and so does John. Oh, it feels like old times.

I look at his face so close to mine.

He is so changed! Taller. Leaner. Darker. Older.

Last night when we gathered for songs and prayers, John Bowen was a boy. But tonight with the moon shining soft through his hair, he is a man.

Tuesday, August 5, 1856

❧

NEAR PRAIRIE CREEK, NEBRASKA

Mormons do not believe in hell. Or at least not in the way other religious people do.

Still, if we're wrong and there really is a hell, I think it must feel exactly like Nebraska in August.

At this moment, I wear a halo of tiny black bugs. They swarm around my head and face. I drip with sweat. It runs down my skin in rivers, especially on my back, where Rose rides.

Oh, to taste cool air right now.

Nebraska air is hot and wet. Not like the air in Port Talbot, which carries the cold bite of the ocean even in summer.

I miss the sea. I wish I could race down to the docks and smell her.

The handcarts ahead of us are slowing down.

What now?

"Did the Widow Rogers lose another one of her cursed chickens again?"

"Mind your language, Charlotte," says Papa.

Rose squirms like a kitten on my back and fusses. We wait. And wait. I can feel the sweat drip from the sides of my face. Truly, I want to scream and pull my hair! Or someone else's hair. Papa shields his eyes from the white sun and stares ahead.

He mumbles something secret into his beard.

"Mind your language, Papa," I say.

"Wagon train ahead!" someone shouts. "Looks like someone in their company has a busted wheel!"

I crane my neck to get a look. Sure enough, we are coming up on a small group of covered wagons. It's not unusual for our large company of three hundred souls to run into smaller gentile groups traveling west to California or Oregon. The people up ahead have money. I can tell because their oxen are well fed. Their wagons are big and heavy with supplies, and the women wear good clothes.

I tug at the bodice of my own faded red dress, which is getting tighter all the time.

Captain Bunker strides over to the wagon train and introduces himself. Some of us cluster nearby and watch. John stands close to me and Rose. I blush and move away.

Sister Roberts clears her throat and begins translating in a loud voice, even though the Bowens all speak English. Sister Bowen's family was from England originally. I try to remember this sometimes when I am busy hating the English. Sister Bowen proves there are good people from every country. I suppose.

"The captain is telling them who we are. He is asking if they need our help. They are settlers out of Missouri—"

"Missouri!" snorts Brother Roberts.

I look at him in surprise. "Is something wrong with Missouri?"

"Haven't you heard of Governor Boggs and his Extermination Order?"

I shake my head.

Brother Roberts looks at me as if I do not have the wit to tie my own bonnet strings. No doubt he will enlighten us. He's very fond of telling us what a great reader he is of books and of periodicals like *The Millennial Star*. Sometimes he acts as though he's the only person in our company who can interpret the Scriptures for the rest of us, but there's a handful who can read and write as well as he can.

I wish one of them were me.

"Governor Boggs decreed that all Mormons must be removed by one means or another from the state of Missouri," Brother Roberts says.

Ellenor waves aside a small cloud of insects and snorts, "Surely not in this country."

Brother Roberts glares at her. "Why not? Joseph Smith died at the hands of an angry mob. In this country."

Ellenor shifts and stares at her dusty feet.

"Is this evil Governor Boggs still alive, Brother Roberts?" I ask in a small voice.

Of course I know that some people do not care for us. There are always a few gentiles who gather to make fun of us as we pass by their town. I remember a group of boys who yelled at Catherine Jones and threw stones at her, and for a minute I was sorry for her.

Papa always shrugs when people here say things and tells me not to mind them. But I do mind.

It's true that I like to be noticed. But not because I'm odd.

When we joined the church in Port Talbot, there were those who thought we were strange. Still, we spoke the same language as our neighbors. Ate the same food. Wore the same clothes and had fathers and uncles and brothers, sometimes even mothers, who worked in the same colliery.

Goodbye to rain every day.

Goodbye to mud after rain every day.

Goodbye to narrow valleys.

Goodbye, Wales . . .

My stomach is suddenly sick with missing my old home. Would Mary Owen feel the same way?

I reach over my shoulder and touch the top of Rose's

black head, just to be sure she is still safe. She mews and snuggles next to me.

"Well, the Extermination Order is ancient history now," says Brother Bowen.

"And maybe our Mormon brothers and sisters were not completely blameless in their dealings with gentile neighbors," says Papa.

Perhaps. But all of us are uneasy as we watch the two captains.

"What are they saying now, Lititia?" Ellenor asks.

"The Yankee captain wants to know where we have stashed our extra wives," John whispers to Papa and me, his breath on my neck.

Papa laughs. "And what does our captain say to that?"

Sister Roberts gasps at whatever it is that Captain Bunker is saying.

"The captain says there are no plural wives in our group. We're too poor to practice polygamy," says John.

Sister Roberts fingers the cameo at her neck. "He called us poor. I cannot believe that our Captain Bunker would say such a thing to strangers!"

Sister Bowen gapes. "That we're poor?"

"Well! Some of us are better off than others," says Sister Roberts.

Sister Bowen's plump cheeks turn the color of apples in autumn. "Look at us, Lititia. Look at yourself. We're pulling our loads like donkeys. Captain Bunker called us poor because we are poor. *All* of us!"

Sister Roberts picks up her skirts and flounces away. Brother Roberts follows solemnly. Everyone is silent.

"Lordy," Sister Bowen finally mumbles. "I'll have to apologize sometime before the sun goes down, I suppose. I'd hate to have ill feelings when we say prayers tonight."

Brother Bowen slips an arm around Sister Bowen's shoulder. "Their losses have been hard for them, Margaret."

"I understand that. But Lititia and her airs and her cameo get the better of me sometimes."

"Losses?" I ask. Papa pretends to give me a stern look because I'm snooping. But he's interested, too. We're alike, after all.

"Brother Roberts is a fine cabinetmaker. People paid him well for his services once, but times changed." Brother Bowen shrugs. "Brother Roberts's skill stopped earning him the money and respect it once did."

"And then the missionaries found him," says Ellenor in a quiet voice unlike her own. "In his dark hour."

Just like they found Mam. I look after Brother and Sister Roberts and remember the way that Sister Roberts always reaches for her cameo. Without even thinking about it.

The way I sometimes reach for Rose now.

In the end the two captains agree to help each other. We fix their wheel, they share their sugar and flour.

It takes longer to fix the wagon wheel than anyone expects. I sit near our handcart and let Rose grasp my pointing finger. She is getting quite good at it now. I love to see her tiny pink fingers curled around my big brown one.

Here's something else about Rose. Her hair has started to fall out on the back of her head, so that she's quite bald there. I was petrified when I noticed. What had I done wrong? Sister Bowen just laughed when I asked. "Plenty of babies lose their first hair. It rubs off when they sleep. Trust me, Charlotte. Your Rose is just fine. She'll grow up to have a head of glorious black hair, just like Mary."

"Charlotte?"

I look up and see John. He is carrying little George Jenkins on his back. Three other small boys tumble around his feet like a litter of puppies.

"Hello, John." It occurs to me that John has grown friendlier with every step we've taken. He's quite popular with the children now.

"There are families in the wagon train. The children want to make some new friends for the day. Will you and Rose come with us?"

John grins. The air around my head swirls.

"Thank you for the invitation," I say, stiff as a tree.

John offers me his hand, which I ignore as I scramble to my feet. Rose lets out an enormous burp.

"Can I at least help you with Rose?"

"No," I say. And then, "Yes."

John cocks his dark head and grins again. "Which is it, Charlotte? No?" He pauses. "Or yes?"

My face is flaming again. John will think I am always the color of boiled beets.

"Yes. I need help strapping Rose to my back."

John lifts George off his shoulders. "Just a minute, my friend," he says when George starts to whimper.

Then he helps me fit Rose into her sling and onto my back. I flinch like a horse that has just been touched on the flank.

"There," he says. John swings George back onto his shoulders as the other children bounce about. "Let's go."

We meet four brothers with hair the color of butter. They look like teams of yellow oxen. The oldest is probably John's age. Before long the younger boys and our children are laughing and chasing one another about.

John and the older boy, whose name is Mathias Keller, strike up a conversation. I'm surprised how much of it I understand.

My English has been improving. Perhaps it is not such a hateful language after all.

"Mathias!" A girl a year or two younger than I emerges from one of the wagons and jumps neatly to the ground.

She is very pretty, with her long wheat-colored braids and a handsome blue dress that is still crisp in spite of being coated with trail dust. She cradles a doll like the one I found and returned on the ship.

Rose makes baby sounds on my back. Little bird noises.

The girl stops in her tracks when she sees us.

"Come here, Rebecca," says Mathias. "Say hello to the Mormons."

She looks me over. Then she wrinkles up her nose as though someone has just forced her to sniff a dead fish.

I see myself through her eyes. Brown as a fig. Dirty. Too large for my hideous dress with the fraying hem. Too stupid to speak her language. Someone strange. Someone foreign.

Different.

Rebecca Keller looks at John and unwrinkles that small nose. She drops her eyes. But not until she shoots him a coy look beneath a dark fringe of lashes. I gasp.

Rebecca smiles. John smiles back. Soon he'll be asking her to dance.

I quiver. This Rebecca is a spoiled one, with her doll and her crisp dress. I imagine her family even has books in their fancy wagon. Books that she can read herself!

But she cannot speak Welsh.

"I'm going now," I say, giving Rose a boost.

"Why?" John asks.

Rebecca pouts in pretty confusion as we speak to each other in our own language.

"I have other things to do. But I would be much obliged if you would tell your new *friend* here that if I had a pair of scissors, I would gladly snip off her long wheat-colored braids and thrash her with them!"

Then I turn around and run, with Rose bouncing on my back.

I work hard to avoid John for the rest of the day. Pushing the handcart. Washing Rose's bottom. Helping the three Elizabeths gather buffalo chips, which Brother Bowen has begun calling meadow muffins. Mending Mam's blue quilt. Trying not to think of Wales and how I yearn to taste salty air.

John catches up with me and Papa at dinner as I scrape a griddle cake from our frying pan. I wish I'd left behind a few of our pots and pans instead of the rest of Mam's quilts in Iowa City. The only useful cooking utensil is a frying pan. All the sisters say so.

"I want to talk to you, Charlotte," he says in a low voice. I can tell he's full of steam because of the way he keeps running his fingers through his hair. He's done that since we were babies.

"Well, I can't stop you," I say, calmly breaking off a piece of griddle cake and stuffing it into my mouth before serving Papa.

"Charlotte!" Papa's mouth drops open. "Where are your manners?"

John looks like he wants to spit fire. If we were still

children, he'd throw me to the ground. Then I'd bounce to my feet and throw *him* to the ground!

"I want to talk to you," he says. "Alone."

Papa looks from me to John to me again.

He looks down at Rose, who is stretched out on Mam's other quilt. "I'll watch over the baby, Charlotte," he says. "You and John should take a walk by the water and cool down."

I glare at Papa. I glare at John. I even glare at Rose, who is busy watching dust motes swirl in a beam of light. I flounce off, aware that Catherine Jones, who eats alone, is watching.

It's not dark yet, but the air already throbs with cricket music. The thick muddy scent of the water fills my nose.

I am walking very fast. John lopes behind.

"Slow down!" he barks.

"No!"

"You are driving me mad!"

"Good."

"What is the matter with you?" he says as he catches up, panting.

I stop and face him down. "Nothing is the matter with me."

"Why did you run away when we were dancing the other night?"

"Because I was tired. Because Rose needed me."

John snorts. "You've been ignoring me."

Now *I* snort. "You've ignored me ever since I volunteered to carry Rose!"

"I was surprised by you that night," John says in a quiet voice.

I'm quiet, too, remembering. It feels as if it happened years and years ago. Was I ever Charlotte without a baby? Charlotte alone?

"Before that you plagued me," I say to John finally. "On the ship. On the train to Iowa City. We used to be friends when we were little, even though we liked to hit each other with sticks."

"Yes," says John. "You taught me how to skip a rock across the water when I was seven."

"Only because you did it so poorly. You threw worse than a girl."

John laughs, which makes me grumpier.

"Stop laughing at me."

John smacks his forehead in frustration. "I'm not laughing at you, Charlotte. Can we please be friends again? That's why I asked you to dance with me the other night."

The air around me hums.

"You've changed," I whisper.

"*You've* changed!"

I know. My legs are longer. And I am growing breasts. I blush, thinking that John may have noticed.

"Why did you leave after we danced?" he asks again.

"Why do you care? There are always other girls to dance with. Like Rebecca Keller." My voice is shaking.

John's mouth pops open. "Rebecca *who*?"

"Keller. The girl from the wagon train today."

John still acts stupid.

"The *very* pretty girl from the wagon train." As if I really need to remind him.

John just stares at me. Then a slow smile spreads across his face, as if he thinks he has just understood something for the very first time. About him. About me.

"Charlotte," he says, "I wanted to dance with *you*."

For the second time that day, I turn and run away. The sound of crickets and water and John laughing fills my ears.

How did running away from John Bowen become my favorite pastime?

The blood pounds in my face by the time I reach camp. I am sweating like Captain Bunker's horse. I almost knock someone over as I race toward Papa and Rose.

It is Thomas Owen. Mary Owen's husband. Rose's father.

When he realizes who I am, he turns and walks in the opposite direction.

I remember Sister Bowen's words the night I offered to care for Rose.

I think I know what kind of a man Thomas Owen is. The day will come when his heart will claim his child.

Well! I doubt it ever will. He'll go off to Cedar City;

hundreds of miles away, and I will be in Ogden, stuck with Rose forever.

I storm back to the handcart. Oh, it will feel delicious to play mumblety-peg tonight!

Only I never get the chance. Too much to do, and now it is past midnight.

Rose still suckles, although her eyes are closed. Soon her lips will stop moving. Soon her head will roll away from Sister Jenkins's breast. Soon watery milk will trickle from the corner of her mouth and she will sleep.

A few minutes pass and all is exactly as I predicted.

"Thank you, Sister Jenkins," I whisper, gathering Rose into my arms.

She doesn't respond. Rosa Jenkins hardly notices—or cares—who feeds at her breast.

Now, here's a strange turn of events. Although it's late, I'm not tired. Not in the least. Too many thoughts race up and down my brain like squirrels in a tree. So I set Rose on my bedroll next to Papa, then step outside.

The prairie is full of fragrance tonight. Different from the ocean's scent, perhaps, but rich and lovely. And then there is the loud music of insects.

I'm tempted to lift my skirts and sway in time to the noise.

Dance tonight, I tell myself. *Dance while there is still time. . . .*

There's no one here to watch me, so why not? And

why not a waltz while I'm at it? They say that Brother Brigham disapproves of waltzing. Too intimate. But since I am waltzing alone, I'm sure Brother Brigham would forgive me.

One, two, three. *Two,* two, three. *Three,* two, three.

Around and around. Beneath a white wheel of stars.

"Charlotte?"

It's Ellenor Lewis, carrying Rose in her arms. "She started to fuss and woke me. I thought I'd help you tend her for a while. I didn't expect to find you"—Ellenor pauses and lifts her eyebrows—"waltzing."

I giggle. So does Ellenor.

"Who are you waltzing with tonight, Miss Charlotte?"

"Nobody," I answer, grateful for the dark that hides my blushes.

Ellenor takes a seat on a log by the tent and gazes down at Rose. I sit next to her.

"You're such a beautiful baby," Ellenor coos as she gently swings Rose in her arms. "Elias and I want one just like you when we get to Salt Lake City."

"Really?"

She looks up at me and nods hard.

"Well, you can have Rose right now."

Ellenor laughs. So do I. It feels good to make a little joke.

"Rose doesn't belong to you," says Ellenor.

"I keep forgetting," I say. "So does Brother Owen."

"Poor little flower," says Ellenor, lightly trailing her

finger down the side of Rose's dark head. I reach over, touch Rose's nose, and smile. Her nose always makes me laugh. I don't know why.

Rose focuses on my face, then closes her eyes.

"You'll miss her when she's gone, Charlotte," Ellenor whispers.

Saturday, August 16, 1856

❦

OUTSIDE NORTH PLATTE, NEBRASKA

"Indians ahead!" someone shouts as we set up camp for the evening.

I shift Rose on my back, put my hand over my brow to block out the light of the setting sun, and search for them.

I think about the sailor on the *S. Curling* and the stories he told about Indians—how they would kill us and take our scalps for trophies.

Well, we've met several parties of Indians since leaving Iowa City. None of them seems interested in our scalps. Instead, they want gifts. They want to trade. They give us coffee and flour and sometimes buffalo meat for a few of our things in return. They also share with Captain Bunker information about the trail ahead.

So the sailor's Indian stories weren't true, which makes me wonder if what he said about mermaids was false as well.

Still, the Indians make me nervous. I hate the way they thunder out of the horizon like a sudden and violent storm.

I see them now, approaching on horseback beneath a cloud of dust. They have painted faces and a single strip of black hair running down the center of their otherwise clean-shaven heads.

Captain Bunker walks out to greet them. The Indians dismount, tie up their horses, and start wandering through our camp, laughing and picking through our things. Captain Bunker has explained that they don't intend to be rude. It's just their way.

Well, I don't care for their way.

One of the braves stops in front of Sister Roberts and touches the cameo at her neck.

"Gift?" he asks. "For me?"

Sister Roberts shrinks back.

"No!"

The rest of the women respond the same way when the Indians touch them. Ellenor tries to smile and laugh, but she draws away just the same.

Only Catherine Jones refuses to flinch when they touch her scar and discuss it among themselves. You would think she does not find it odd to have a strange man touch her.

I watch the Indians examine one of Sister Bowen's quilts.

Please, God. I will repent all my sins soon—tonight!—if you will make them leave me and Papa and Rose and all our things alone.

I fumble through the handcart, looking for utensils to use for the evening meal and perhaps to offer if I am asked to trade. As long as they do not want my frying pan.

Rose wakes up and cries.

"Shhh, baby girl."

Rose still whimpers, so I place my mouth close to the tiny bud of her ear and whisper the words of our song.

"We're going to a new place,
a safe place,
a place for us to play
and a place for us to grow,
a place where girls will tend their houses
and their gardens dressed with roses!"

My stomach is rolling.

A brave. He sorts through the possessions in our handcart and drags out Mam's yellow quilt. "Gift? For me?"

The quilt flaps in the breeze like a banner. The Indian smiles at me. Even though he is young, most of his teeth are gone. The rest look like dry kernels of corn.

I snatch the quilt from his hands. "No!"

He moves toward to me. Closer. Closer still. I can feel his breath on my cheek.

"I give good present for you," he says, still smiling, and lifts a strand of my wild hair. Then he reaches over my shoulder and touches Rose.

I step back. He will not touch her again!

A frown steals across his face.

Papa is by my side. He takes the hat off his head and hands it to the brave. "Present." He says the word in English. "For you."

"No, Papa," I whisper. "The sun will fry you."

Papa ignores me and smiles at the brave. The Indian drops Papa's hat square on his head and smiles back. Then he digs into a pouch that dangles from his side, pulls something out, and places it in the palm of Papa's hand.

A woman's garnet ring. The red stone winks at me like an evil red eye. The sight of it makes me sick. How did the brave get this ring?

Already I think I know the story.

A beautiful young woman is traveling alone late at night. Out of nowhere, Indians appear. They kill her and slide the ring from her pale white finger. . . .

Captain Bunker invites the Indians to eat supper with us. They stay until dark. I try not to look at the brave who sits at the fire, laughing hard and wearing Papa's hat.

Then, as suddenly as they came, they leave.

Riding fast and hard beneath the evening's new stars.

"George!" Sister Jenkins cries as we count off and prepare to go to our tents for the night. "George is gone!"

A cry goes up. Before long, we are all searching for George.

"It is a wonder she has not lost the boy before now," I hear Brother Roberts say. "I never saw a mother who looked after her children less."

I hate to agree with Brother Roberts, but he's right. Sister Jenkins wanders through camp each night with empty eyes.

"You're wrong, Husband."

My mouth pops open. Can Sister Roberts really be contradicting her holy husband?

"She was a fine mother before her husband died," says Sister Roberts.

"George! Georgie!" Sister Jenkins's frantic voice rings throughout the camp.

An ugly thought starts to form in my head as I poke through surrounding bushes, searching for George and praying I will not disturb a snake. The Indians. What if they kidnapped George? Things like this have happened before. Not to us. But I've heard stories.

I reach over my shoulder and touch Rose's hair.

Stealing a child is easy when you know how. . . .

I feel the blood pound behind my eyes. If I ever find this wicked man, I will—

Someone is shouting. "Here he is! Sound asleep in the wrong tent beneath a pile of blankets!"

I run in the direction of the shouting, just in time to see Sister Jenkins barrel into the tent. Minutes later she emerges with George, covering his head with kisses the way she did that day on the ship. George is rubbing his eyes.

He was fine all along.

I let out a deep breath and feel limp. I walk in the direction of our handcart, kicking a loose stone as I go.

How could I have gotten everything so wrong?

In my head I see the Indian's yellow teeth. My skin remembers the feel of his hot breath. He was so . . . different.

Rose lets out a halfhearted cry. I whisper and coo, and I keep thinking about Rebecca Keller. The girl with the light yellow braids who once looked down upon a certain Welsh girl because she was different, too.

So now it's late and I'm lying here in a hot swirl of blankets, not sleeping. Not sleeping is becoming a habit for me.

"Charlotte?" Papa whispers. "Is Rose keeping you awake?"

I look at Rose, snuggled between Papa and me like a little black-and-white rabbit.

"She's fine," I say.

Papa reaches across Rose to take my hand. But tonight his rough skin does not comfort me.

"How do you think that Indian came by the ring he gave you?" I ask.

Papa laughs softly. "The same way he came by my hat, Charlotte. He traded something else for it. And someday we'll probably have to trade it away, too. I suspect that ring may turn into a blessing for you and me and this baby before we reach Utah."

Papa squeezes my hand before letting it go. Then he rolls over and goes straight to sleep.

You can do that when your conscience is easy.

Sleep . . .

Monday, August 18, 1856

❧

Near Ash Hollow, Nebraska

Clouds of dust hang thick and heavy over the prairie. The sound of pounding hooves fills the hot air like the roar of an ocean.

Papa lets out a low whistle as we stop to watch buffalo running in the distance.

"How many of them would you say are out there this time?" Brother Bowen asks as his family joins us.

Papa reaches to push his hat back on his head, then remembers it is no longer there. "Thousands."

"I've never seen so many at once," says Sister Bowen, her voice shot through with awe.

Although they're far away from us, I can feel the

ground tremble beneath my feet. My body vibrates as buffalo storm the prairie.

They're quick animals, in spite of their bulk, and when they run in a herd, they look like an endless rolling wave washing across the long Nebraska grass.

"Do you think the men will be allowed to hunt this time?" John asks.

We're careful about killing the buffalo so we won't anger the Indians. But my mouth is hungry for the rich dark taste of meat.

"We can only hope," says Sister Bowen.

"*Stampede!*" A shout goes up.

I turn to Papa. "Stampede? But the buffalo are miles away from here!"

One of the company's teamsters, Brother Grant, gallops toward us on horseback.

"You!" he says to John as he reins in his bay. "We need you." He thrusts out his arm for John to grab. A surprised but pleased look flashes across John's face.

"What's going on?" shouts Brother Bowen as John scrambles onto the back of the horse.

"The sound of the buffalo spooked the milk cows. They're stampeding. We need men and boys to head them off."

The teamster digs his heels into his horse's sides, turns, and races away. I know John Bowen is smiling.

It would be such a fine adventure to chase down a

company of cows while buffalo thundered in the distance, to be riding on that horse with the wind blowing in my face and through my hair.

Instead of standing here with a baby strapped to my back.

"Look at this pattern, Charlotte," says Elizabeth the Jolly. She's lining up my glass beads on Mam's yellow quilt, where Rose lies examining her own hands.

I've decided to make myself a necklace I can wear now instead of saving my beads for a fancy purse. I asked the three Elizabeths to help me design it while John Bowen chases the runaway cows.

But they all want different things. Elizabeth the Musical wants me to put like colors together. Blacks first. Then reds. Then blues. Then ambers.

Elizabeth the Fair thinks I should string three of each until I have used up all the beads. Three ambers. Three blues. Three reds. Three blacks. Three ambers again.

And now Elizabeth the Jolly is suggesting one red, one black, one amber, one blue—

Rose lets out a little cry.

Elizabeth the Jolly scoots over by Rose's side and peers into the baby's face. "Is she hungry, Charlotte?"

I shake my head. "She's wet."

The girls all look at me in surprise. Then they laugh.

"But how can you tell?" asks Elizabeth the Jolly.

"You have a baby brother. Can't you tell the difference between a hungry cry and a wet cry?"

She giggles. "No! I only know that he disturbs my sleep at night!"

I smile. "Rose has all kinds of cries. Tired cries. Bored cries. Frustrated. Frightened."

"You're making it up," says Elizabeth the Musical.

"I'm not!" I laugh.

They look down at Rose in wonder as she stretches out her long neck and rolls her head from side to side.

"She thinks it feels good not to be bound up in a sling this afternoon," I say. "You can tell by the way she's moving."

Elizabeth the Fair smiles at me. "Just see how much you know, Charlotte!"

I shrug.

I wish I were riding with John.

I'm wearing my new necklace as the three Elizabeths and I sneak away to play in the river by early moonlight, while Ellenor and Elias Lewis stroll through camp with Rose tucked in Ellenor's arms, making plans for the day they have their own babies.

When we get to the river's edge, we glance around to make sure we're alone. Then we strip down and plunge into the water as fireflies weave glowing patterns above us.

Elizabeth the Jolly squeals.

"Hush," I say. "Sister Roberts will hear us and make us come back for prayers and song."

"I like prayers and song," says Elizabeth the Musical.

"We all like prayers and song," I say, "just not every single night."

I grin and splash water at her. She squeals with laughter and splashes me back, and before long all of us are spitting water and dunking one another as if we were John and Morgan.

"Look at my muscles now that I have pushed a handcart across the prairie!" Elizabeth the Jolly curls her arms and makes muscles pop into view.

"Mine are bigger!" says Elizabeth the Fair.

"Mine are!" Elizabeth the Musical makes her muscles bulge.

So do I.

"We will frighten our husbands with our huge muscles someday!" Elizabeth the Jolly says. Then she roars like a lion and we all laugh.

"Lizzie!" It's Elizabeth the Fair's mam, standing on the riverbank with several sisters from her tent.

Elizabeth the Fair gulps. "How long have you been there, Mam?"

"Long enough. Out of the water, girls. Time for bed. And don't forget when you kneel tonight to repent for stealing away and leaving the rest of us behind."

We scramble out of the river, dry off, wring water from our braids, and pull on our dusty clothes.

As we walk back to camp, we hear a whoop and a splash and much laughter as Elizabeth the Fair's mam and her friends leap like girls into the murky water.

Friday, August 22, 1856

e∾

Between Ash Hollow and
Chimney Rock, Nebraska

Night.

Rose lets out sharp cries and pulls her knees to her chest.

She's hungry. I have suspected for a long time now that she isn't getting enough milk, although Sister Jenkins nurses Rose as often and as long as she nurses her Emma.

Poor Sister Jenkins. So thin, she's disappearing before our eyes.

Looking for something to eat, Rose stuffs her hand into her mouth and gums it hard. Soon she will cry in disappointment. Papa mutters in his sleep. Someone coughs. Someone else does, too.

Coughing makes me nervous.

Dear God, please protect Rose from coughing and all manner of sickness.

Although the night is warm, I bundle up Rose in her blanket. The two of us slip outside. A breeze lifts my hair and I look up.

I've never seen real pearls, only heard them described. I think this moon above me right now must look like a pearl—round and fat and white. It casts a fat pearl's light, making the world around me glow silver. I think of the words of the prophet Joseph that Mam made me learn by heart.

The earth rolls upon her wings, and the sun giveth his light by day, and the moon giveth her light by night, and the stars also give their light, as they roll upon their wings in their glory, in the midst of the power of God.

Here's something I remember about Mam—the way her face was lit with fire when she first said these words to me. Mam had found someone who read them to her over and over until she could say them for herself.

"You understand what this means, don't you?" Mam said. "The prophet Joseph called the sun 'him' and the moon 'her.' That means they're alive. The stars, too. The whole world breathes, Charlotte. Just like you and me."

Mam turned her head to look out the window. She smiled her secret smile. "I've always known it," she said, more to herself than to me. "Deep in my bones I have always known it."

I love the words of the prophet Joseph, too. For the way they sound as much as for what they say.

I pull Rose close to my heart. She reaches up and touches my lips with tiny fingers.

I miss Mam tonight. There are certain questions I need to ask her. For instance, I would very much like to know more about the messy bleeding that started up after my birthday. Maybe if Mam had been there, I wouldn't have been so scared when it began. But all I could think of was the night Sister Mary Owen bled to death, and I secretly wondered if I was going to die, too.

Who would look after Papa if I did that? Or Rose?

Then Sister Bowen explained that it was normal and told me how to take care of myself.

It would also be nice to know something about breasts. Mine are mostly a nuisance. They are often tender, especially at night when I roll over on my stomach. My poor dress is tighter than ever.

I could talk to Papa about breasts, I suppose. I talk to him about everything else. But I'd rather crawl backward to Zion on my hands and knees than do that.

Rose's fingers are in my mouth now. I do love the way they taste.

"Oh, Mam," I whisper. "I wish you were here."

Rose gurgles. Such a healthy sound. A happy sound! I laugh and sing our song.

"We're going to a new place,
a safe place,
a place for us to play

and a place for us to grow,
a place where girls will tend their houses
and their gardens dressed with roses!"

Rose stares at my face, then begins closing her eyes, closing . . . so near to sleep. She looks away suddenly. Is something out there? I turn.

A woman, dressed completely in white, stands in the moonlight at the edge of camp. I cannot see her face because she is looking away from our tents and handcarts and livestock in the direction of the next day's walk.

Although I'm startled, I am not afraid. She's a fellow traveler, with loose shining hair, in a nightgown, looking ahead to tomorrow's journey.

"Hello there," I call out.

Slowly, slowly she glances back over her shoulder. She looks at Rose. She looks at me.

And then she slips away, into the shadows.

Saturday, August 23, 1856

❧

"I can't fix supper and bounce you on my hip at the same time," I say to Rose, who lies squirming and squalling on Mam's flax-colored quilt.

I wish someone were here to soothe her. Either that or jam my sore ears with cotton so I don't have to listen to her. But Papa is helping the other men pitch the tent for tonight. Sister Bowen nurses one of the sisters who is ill. Ellenor and Elias have stolen away for a stroll in the evening heat. Sister Roberts reads her Scripture. Sister Jenkins is next to useless. Which leaves Catherine Jones to help me.

Catherine Jones hold Rose?

Ha!

I poke at the griddle cake bubbling in the pan and wish

with all my heart it were meat. I thought I was hungry on the ship, but that was nothing compared with how hungry I am now. At least on the ship we often had chicken to eat, even if I didn't always get my fill. For a moment I close my eyes and remember the scent of roast chicken.

Oh, I am hungry. And weary, too. My bones ache.

Rose never did sleep last night.

I look at her on the quilt now, screwing up her little red face and battering me with her screams.

I jab at the griddle cake. How is it possible for such a small girl to be so much trouble?

Rose started crying again after the White Lady left last night.

The two of us stayed outside the tent until birds chattered and the sun exploded out of the eastern prairie. I held Rose and paced. Back and forth. Back and forth. Still that baby kept on fussing. Just not as much as if we'd been lying down.

Here's something I've learned about babies. They're happier when they're moving. Which means you're required to keep moving, too!

When will this cursed griddle cake be done? I spear it again. And again.

I could just kill that worthless Brother Owen. I think I will take this fork and stick it in him. After that, I will crown him with this heavy frying pan. This heavy *hot* frying pan!

"Ha! Ha!" I will say.

Brother Owen does not bother to ask about his screaming Rose. Ever. Instead, he brings up the rear of our procession by day and skulks around camp like a whipped dog by night. He keeps his distance from me, afraid that I'll thrust Rose into his arms and say, "Here!"

I cannot believe his shoulders once reminded me of Papa's shoulders.

I have a new plan for my life now, one that I formed this afternoon while pushing the handcart as Rose squirmed upon my back. I'll say no to the man who asks me to marry him. That way I will not have Roses of my own. Already I can tell you the story of how I did not marry and how I did not have children.

A handsome young man whose name isn't John comes to visit me in Papa's home in Salt Lake City. It's the big house. Next to Brigham Young's. He carries flowers and Welsh love spoons that he has carved with his own hands. Rose and I are sitting on the porch.

"Charlotte Edwards," he cries, "I cannot live without you! Kiss me and marry me!"

I give him a smile that is both sweet and sad. Disappoint him I must.

"I'm grateful for your offer, sir," I say. "Truly. But I've chosen not to marry."

He tries to change my mind. Papa tries to change my mind. Rose tries to change my mind. But I am firm.

He'll find someone else with whom to share the love spoons, although I don't think he'll forget me.

I hope he won't forget me.

Of course, I don't wish to be the solitary Catherine Jones. But after last night and today, I begin to see the wisdom of her choice. No husband, no children.

The griddle cake sizzles and turns deep gold around the edge. Done. I remove the pan from the fire. Rose screams. I drop our supper.

"Rose!"

She stops for a second, startled by my voice. Then she screams even more loudly.

"Charlotte! Come see what we've made!"

Hyrum, Jacob, and Mary skip toward me, swinging their arms. I wonder if they still have the beads we found in the anthill together.

I look at the griddle cake at my feet, coated with dust. So much has changed since that day I danced with ants in my hair.

"Please, Charlotte. Come with us." Mary tugs my skirt. Her eyes are brown and pleading.

Oh, it would feel good to play again. I kick the griddle cake and send it sailing like a pig's bladder filled with air. What will Papa and I eat tonight? I don't know. I don't care.

I lift Rose and follow the children. They take me to something they've constructed out of rocks and grass and twigs.

"It's our village," says Hyrum.

"Here's the church. Here are the houses and the farms," says Jacob.

"What is the name of your village?" I ask over the sound of Rose's screams.

"Deseret," says Mary.

At the edge of Deseret there are trenches lined with pebbles and filled with crickets.

I point and cock an eyebrow.

"Those are the horses and cows," says Hyrum.

"And pigs," says Mary.

I laugh and so does someone behind me. John. The late-afternoon light shines warm behind him. My heart beats faster.

"Hello, Charlotte," he says.

I nod. Why am I so shy? Why do things have to change?

Jacob and Hyrum whoop and leap on John. Mary giggles. And so do I. My laugh is different. It sounds high and strange in my own ears.

"Tell me the names of your livestock," John says.

The children all talk at once.

"Book of Mormon names—"

"Nephi and Lehi—"

"Alma and Ammon—"

"Samuel and Moroni—"

"Wicked King Noah—"

I like the story of King Noah and how he burns God's prophet Abinadi at the stake, because, quite frankly, it is more exciting than some of the other stories in the Book of Mormon.

John gets down on his hands and knees to examine every rock and stick of Deseret. Mary is so pleased by his attention that her cheeks turn pink.

Meanwhile, a small miracle happens. Rose lets out one last gusty cry, shudders, and falls asleep in my arms. Her head is drenched with sweat from crying.

And I am drenched with sweat from listening.

John stands and brushes the dust from his pants. "Thank you for showing me your village," he says to the children. "Now Charlotte and I are going for a walk down by the river. Alone. Except for Rose." John smiles at me.

My heart skips a beat.

"I think it would be better for Rose if I left her here with someone so she can nap," I say.

Only there's no one who can help me, which I realize as soon as John and Rose and I return to my family's handcart. They're all busy still. Except for one person, who should be busier.

Anger prickles the back of my neck.

Thomas Owen! Oh, the lazy limping ox! I hate him!

I stoop and lay Rose gently on Mam's quilt, which is still spread out on the ground. "I think we should leave her here in the shade of the handcart. Papa will return soon to watch over her."

John furrows his brow. "Are you sure?"

"I leave her alone all the time," I lie.

John smiles at me. For as long as I live, I think I will remember how he looked at me.

We walk downstream, away from camp. In this spot the North Platte is bordered with trees whose high branches drape shade over river and stone. Everything around us is green and silver. Quiet, too, except for the singing of birds and the noise of water. This place feels old. Ancient. As if it has always been this way and it will always be this way.

John and I search for rocks and fill our pockets. John is good at skipping rocks. But then, he had an excellent teacher.

"Strange," John says as he tosses a stone from one hand to the other. "This reminds me of home."

"Me too."

"Do you ever miss Wales, Charlotte?"

"Sometimes, although I think it's Mam I really miss. Do you miss Wales?"

"No!" John throws a fierce glance over his shoulder, as though he can see Wales now, shrouded in clouds and rising from the distant sea.

"I am free here," he says. "I can stand up straight. Stretch out my arms and legs. Look up whenever I choose and see the sun. You have no idea what it is like to go for days and days without seeing the sun because you are buried in the belly of a mine."

John is right. I can't imagine it. Nor do I want to now that I have lived on these wide prairies and watched the sun move through the day.

"Papa took me to work with him the morning I turned thirteen," he says. "I felt proud of myself as I walked to the colliery with him. I was a man. Just like Papa. Just like my brothers, Evan and Thomas.

"By the time Papa and I reached the pithead, I was sick with excitement. I couldn't wait to enter the mines with the rest of the men. I stepped into the crowded pit cage, waiting to be lowered to the bottom.

"They dropped us nearly a quarter of a mile.

"The ride was fast and hard and dark. Bits of dust and coal blew into my face. Wind whistled in my ears. I screamed, Charlotte. In front of all of them. When we stopped, the others in the pit cage teased me. They called me a Mormon girl."

"They were only having fun with you," I say.

John shrugs. "I hated the deep darkness of the pit and the way it smothers a soul like a filthy blanket. I hated tasting dust and slithering on my stomach through tight places. And I hated myself for hating it all. For being afraid.

"Why couldn't I be like my father? Or my brothers? Sure of myself. Things are always so clear to them. Black is black. White is white. Angels speak to men.

"These feelings I have inside of me, Charlotte— sometimes they make me hard to be around."

I remember one day on the ship. How John stole my chess piece. How Brother Bowen wondered what was troubling his son.

"You have always been hard to be around," I point out with a smile.

John grins at me, then grows serious again.

"Even if I hadn't believed a single word of it—that Joseph Smith was a prophet and that the Book of Mormon is the word of God—I would have said that I did. I would have said anything to leave my life there and come to America."

I can tell that John has never said these words to anyone before. Not even to himself. I nod.

Your words are safe with me, I say to him in my head. *You are safe with me.*

"Even though what we are doing is hard—the pushing, the pulling, the heat, the trail dust, the insects—it's better than the colliery. I won't have to be a collier in Zion, Charlotte. I won't have to work like my father or my brothers."

"In America you can be a king if you want to," I say.

John laughs. He takes the rock he has been tossing up and down and throws it into the water.

Splash!

Then he charges like a bull into the river, fully dressed, and climbs onto a wet rock. He stretches out his arms and throws back his head. His hair sparkles with water.

"I'm King John of America!" he roars.

I laugh as I hitch up my skirts and leap into the water myself.

"Mad King John!" I whoop as I join him.

Oh, it feels good to have the dust washed from my shoes and my clothes and my skin.

"Do you still think you can skip rocks better than I can?" he asks.

"Of course."

We dig into our pockets and let stones fly. John's rocks hit the water and sink.

"I told you!" I shove John off the rock and leap into the water after him. Soaking wet, we scrounge on the river's floor for more rocks.

"I need more lessons," John says. "Obviously."

"Obviously."

We crawl out of the river and plop down on the bank.

I am so happy right now. Happy for the sight of tall trees and water. Happy for the feel of cool air and the smell of bark and wet leaves. Happy for the music in John's voice.

John stands and stretches forth an arm. "King John commands the Lady Charlotte to teach him the proper way to skip a rock."

"Commands?" I say, leaning back on bent elbows.

John looks at me. "Should I plead my case? Would that please my Lady Charlotte?"

Overhead a flock of birds bursts from the trees and fans into strange formations overhead. The sudden beauty of it moves my heart. Slowly I stand up in my dripping dress so John and I are face to face.

"Just ask, John."

The two of us stand very, very still. The air between us hums. Then John bows deeply, in this kingdom of green leaves and water.

Good things. Bad things. This, too, will pass.

Papa's words return to me as John and I sit near the river, playing mumblety-peg with our knives. I am good. But John's better. Much better now that I have begun to worry (just a little) about Rose. If I'm not careful, I'll throw my knife straight into John's shin.

"We should go back," I say finally, pulling my knife out of the ground.

John nods and picks up his own shining blade. Something captures his attention. Another stone.

"Ah! Look at this one, Charlotte."

The stone has some strange design carved into it, as though the stone were a mound of butter, molded and stamped.

"I've seen one of these before," he says. He points at the delicate grooves in the rock. "You see this pattern? It looks like bones. A skeleton of something."

I squint and see the secret pattern for myself.

"This is like looking for shapes in clouds," I say, "only better."

I look up at the clouds now but see only sky. Endless sky stretching over endless sage and yellow prairie. Although the day is warm, I shiver.

"I feel like a dot in the middle of a map."

John nods.

I look at the stone in his hand again. "Do you think anyone will remember us?"

John digs a hole in the earth with the toe of his wet boot. "I never thought about it."

"I don't want to be forgotten," I say. "I don't want to forget. But I do."

Rose! I have forgotten Rose.

I turn and run back to camp so fast I fear my heart will burst. John gallops through the long grasses behind me.

John looks for his father and I look for mine when we reach camp.

I find Papa leaning against the handcart, sharpening his own knife. He greets me with a sunny smile. "There you are, Charlotte." He looks over my shoulder. "Where's Rose?"

My heart shimmies up my throat. "She isn't here? With you?"

The smile slips from Papa's face. "No."

My stomach begins to churn. My hands turn moist. I dash to the other side of the handcart, where I left Rose in the shade not so very long ago. . . .

My heart pounds as I circle the handcart. My throat closes, so that I cannot breathe. Tiny stars flash in front of my eyes, as though I've been hit in the head.

Gone!

"Charlotte." Papa stops sharpening his knife. "Where's the baby?"

He sounds like God himself on Judgment Day.

"Papa, I've done a dreadful thing. What if the wolves have carried her away?" I begin to sob.

Papa sets down his knife, takes me by the shoulders, and gives me a good shake. "Stop behaving like a child and tell me what's happened."

The whole sorry tale tumbles out as tears slide down my cheeks.

Papa frowns. "I had no idea you were struggling so with Rose. You seemed to be managing so well. All the sisters say so."

My mouth pops open.

"I should have noticed," says Papa as he folds me to his chest. I cling to his shirt until he gently pushes me away. "Perhaps one of them has her now."

Papa heads north. I head south, trotting through camp, kicking up dirt and pebbles as I go. I run into Ellenor Lewis, who sits on a log pulling prickly-pear needles out of her feet.

Ellenor grins at me. "Was that you and Brother John I saw stealing away together? Will there be Welsh wedding spoons for the two of you in Salt Lake City?"

"Have you seen Rose?"

Ellenor shakes her head. "I have not seen your sweet flower baby."

I swallow down my panic and leave Ellenor tending to her cut and dirty toes. I pick up my wet skirts so they won't trail in the dust and start to run. My soggy shoes slap the ground.

"What in the world . . ." I run headlong into Sister Roberts's bosom. Her chin quivers.

"Begging your pardon, Sister Roberts, but have you seen my Rose?"

She draws in a sharp breath of air. "Rose?"

"I left her sleeping by the handcart," I say. I pick up the hem of my apron in spite of myself and start twisting it again like a nervous little girl. "When I returned, she was gone."

"You left her?" Sister Roberts spits the words in my face. Miserable, I nod.

"Don't you know that you should never ever leave a child alone?"

I nod again. Ordinarily I would hate Sister Roberts for lecturing me like this. But in the dark pit of my sick heart, I know she's right.

"We'll find her, we'll find her," Sister Roberts says. "I'll go this way. Go!"

Where is Rose? Think, Charlotte, think!

A thought begins to sprout in my brain. What if Rose woke up hungry while I was visiting with John down by the river? Made a fuss? Wouldn't someone have taken her to Sister Jenkins?

I find Sister Rosa Jenkins with Emma and George at the ragged edge of camp. Emma and George are rolling around on the ground, so that they're coated with dust. Even the mucus trailing from George's tiny nose is shot through with dirt.

Sister Jenkins sits apart. She stares at the prairie ahead.

"First the ocean. Now this. Miles and miles of nothing leading nowhere," she says as I approach. "My husband didn't tell me it would be like this."

"Sister Jenkins?"

She looks at me. The flesh beneath her dull eyes is loose and dark. The hollows in her cheeks are deep. "I do not wish to take another step."

A better girl wouldn't feel the way I do right now. She would pity Sister Jenkins. Hold her and comfort her. Offer to help with Emma and George as we drag our handcarts over this endless ocean of grass.

Instead I want to grab Sister Rosa Jenkins by her boney shoulders and shake her until the rest of her pale hair tumbles into her face.

She doesn't wish to do this anymore? Well, what choice does she have? What choice does anybody have?

I look at little George. When was the last time Sister Jenkins combed his hair? Washed his hands? Sang to him as he drifted to sleep? Wiped his nose?

Oh, when was the last time Sister Rosa Jenkins thought about anything besides her own cursed misery?

"I'm looking for Rose, Sister Jenkins," I manage to say.

Her hands begin to move restlessly, as though she is knitting air.

I repeat myself.

"Rose?"

"Yes!" I snap. "Rose. *My baby!*"

George stops rolling around on the ground and looks up at me, surprised. Sister Jenkins, her hands still in motion, stares back over the prairie. Miles and miles of nothing. A light breeze bends the grass and lifts her hair. I stomp away.

"Catherine Jones has her," Sister Jenkins calls after me in a weak voice. "She brought me Rose to feed not too long ago."

I exhale a whistle. When did Catherine Jones become interested in babies?

I stride through camp until I find her standing next to a basket filled with sewing supplies and socks that need darning. Her back is to me. She sways gently, like a dark and slender tree. I hear her singing in a language I do not understand. Casting a spell.

"Sister Jones?"

She turns, holding Rose. Catherine Jones is smiling.

The smile slips from her face.

I square my shoulders and lift my chin, although my heart batters the cage of my chest.

"I have come for my baby girl, Sister Jones."

"Your baby girl?" Can there really be a hint of a smile around her lips?

"Yes." I take large steps toward her as if I were Papa. I thrust out my arms. "Thank you for watching over her, but I won't be leaving my baby alone again."

Still cradling Rose, Catherine Jones stares at me. Then she smiles down on Rose, who stretches a hand toward Catherine Jones's face. Catherine sings to her again in that strange language.

It cannot be a curse. It is far too beautiful.

"An old Gaelic lullaby," Catherine Jones says to me when she finishes her song. "My mam sang it to me when I was little."

I don't look away when she says this or when she looks at me closely. Then, as if I have passed some mysterious test, she hands me my Rose.

"I found her crying, Charlotte, so I picked her up and held her. Your Rose makes me remember the feel of a child. She's a fair one, all right."

I let out a huge breath and nod hard, grateful that Catherine Jones isn't scolding me.

"She's very pretty for a baby, isn't she, Sister Jones? Sometimes I look at Emma Jenkins, with her bald head, and feel sorry for her because she is not Rose."

I smooth down Rose's cloud of dark, dark hair and laugh because I am so happy that she is fine.

"All is well!" I want to shout at the birds above me. "All is well!"

Catherine Jones laughs, too. Her laughter sounds like bells. "Emma Jenkins will no doubt have beautiful moon-colored hair like her mam someday, Charlotte."

"That may be true. But she will never ever be as beautiful as Rose."

"I agree," says Catherine Jones. "I favor dark babies myself."

I take Rose's small hand and kiss her fingers. One by one by one.

Rose looks up at me. And smiles!

I gasp, then kiss her fingers again. She smiles again.

"Did you see her smile, Sister Jones?"

Catherine Jones smiles herself and nods. "You watch. Now that your Rose knows how to smile, people will be standing on their heads to get her to do it again."

I laugh. I can see Papa standing on his head now!

"Charlotte," says Catherine Jones, "this is important. Listen to me."

I look up from my Rose's smiling face.

"If you need help, ask me. I know something of babies and their ways."

I swallow. "Thank you."

Catherine Jones has just offered me her friendship, too.

Thursday, August 28, 1856

❧

CHIMNEY ROCK, NEBRASKA

"I believe we're almost there now, Charlotte," says Papa.

He's talking about Chimney Rock, a huge tower of colored rock that looms ahead of us like the turret of a castle.

It has seemed close for a long time now. Close enough to touch, to kiss with the palm of your hand. But no. We just keep grunting and groaning and toiling over this dreary trail.

And *still* Chimney Rock stands on the horizon, just ahead.

I'm dying to reach this Chimney Rock. Captain Bunker has promised that we'll stop and explore. He says there are names carved into the stone. Names of the people who've gone before us. He says he even knows some of the people and can locate their names easily. It will be so interesting to see all those names. It makes you feel as if people actually finish this journey.

Also, I want to get to Chimney Rock because I'm weary of walking with the three Elizabeths.

They asked to join me and Papa this morning because their own families didn't need them. And we had some good fun together. At first.

We sang "The Handcart Song" and roared so loudly when we got to the chorus that Brother Roberts reminded us that God does not approve of loudness.

"For some must push and some must pull
As we go marching up the hill;
So merrily on the way we go
Until we reach the Valley-o!"

I didn't say anything. But I'm sure that "Thou shalt not annoy grumpy Brother Roberts" isn't one of the original Ten Commandments. So I just sang that much more loudly whenever the Elizabeths and I got close to his handcart.

The three Elizabeths helped me with Rose for a while. They took turns cooing at her and making faces and even carrying her a little way. But then they lost interest, which is what always happens.

It makes me laugh when I think about it. These girls

want to marry handsome bishops and be mothers someday. But they don't know the first true thing about having
your own baby to take care of.

So I started to tire of being with the Elizabeths. Also,
they started to talk about some of the boys in our group.

And now they're talking about John.

"He's just so handsome!" Elizabeth the Fair sighs.

"Even if Papa says he is a wild one," Elizabeth the
Musical coos.

Elizabeth the Jolly sweeps her hand to her forehead
like an actress on a theater poster. "I just want to faint
whenever I see him."

She flings out her arms, closes her eyes, and falls back
into the other Elizabeths' arms. Have they been practic-
ing swoons together?

They giggle. I try to smile but feel my cheeks turn
pink instead.

"He's *my* John," I want to say, "and I don't wish to
share him."

Really, how can two women share one man? Maybe it
helps if you don't like him much but think he's useful
when it comes to chopping firewood. I once overheard
the Widow Rogers say she wouldn't mind marrying a
polygamist when she gets to Utah because then she'd
have other women to help her put up with the burden of
living with a man.

I can't imagine feeling that way.

"I'll race you up Chimney Rock when we get there, Charlotte," someone whispers over my shoulder.

It's John. He's come up behind me and gotten close to see if I'll startle. But I don't give him the satisfaction.

"I'll beat you to the top with or without Rose on my back," I say.

The three Elizabeths look shocked. Whether by the sudden sight of John standing close to me or by the sound of my words, it's hard to say exactly.

"You won't catch yourself a boyfriend if you talk like that, Charlotte," says Elizabeth the Jolly, with a sideways look at John that says *she* wouldn't talk to him that way.

John laughs, and suddenly I want to slap him.

Why is he so friendly, so happy, so handsome, that he can turn girls into stupid geese right before my eyes?

But then he winks at me. Just me.

I feel better at once.

"Here, Charlotte," Papa says after securing our hand-cart. "Why don't I take Rose so you can ramble up the rock with the others?"

"Come with us," I say.

Papa grins and holds my chin between his fingers. "Believe me, I've had enough of walking for one day, Daughter. I'm happy to sit for a while."

Why would someone *sit* instead of climbing up Chimney Rock?

Papa puts his big bear hands on my shoulders, spins me around, and loosens Rose's sling. He takes her in his arms, kisses her forehead, and shoos me away.

"Enjoy yourself," Papa says.

John and I scramble up the base of Chimney Rock like goats. The three Elizabeths started out with us, but they couldn't keep up. Ah. Such a pity.

John pauses. Although I'd never let him know it, I'm gasping for air.

"Look here, Charlotte," he says, running his finger across a flat surface of stone. "Another name."

I move closer to examine it for myself.

A small familiar pain touches my heart. I feel it each time I see a sign or a newspaper or a book—or a name scratched here into Chimney Rock.

My eyebrows knit together.

John starts talking, tracing the pattern of the letters as he does. "I wonder what this one says. Not 'John.' I can read my own name, at least."

John grins, rumples his hair, and glances over at me.

"Did you just eat something very sour, Charlotte?" he asks. "Is that why you look exactly like our Sister Roberts?"

"I look like Sister Roberts?"

He nods and I pull a face at him.

"Well? What's the matter, then?"

I fold my arms across my chest and let out a sigh. "Do you ever wish you could read and write?"

John squints at me, then looks away and shrugs. "I don't think about it much."

"Not even when Brother Roberts reads Scripture to us in the morning? Don't you wish you could read those Scriptures for yourself?"

John flashes me a crooked smile. "That thought has never crossed my mind. I'm happy to have other people tell me what's there."

I feel a small breath of disappointment.

"I'm sorry if you don't like my answer," says John.

I look at him, quick as a bird. Does he read my very thoughts?

He continues. "But I don't see why you can't learn how to read for yourself someday. We're in America now. Not Wales. Anything can happen here. Right?"

I nod slowly. Perhaps all things really are possible in the Promised Land.

"Come on," says John. "Let's keep going."

I look out and see miles and miles of plains below. I look to the east and see where we've been. I look to the west and see where we're going.

"Go ahead, John," I say. "I want to be by myself for a little while."

One thing you don't have much of on the trail is time alone.

John hesitates. I smile a smile that says *Go on, I am fine.* So he turns and runs up the mountainside. But not until he points at a lone figure standing a distance away from us on the rocks. It's Catherine Jones, looking eastward. She's unpinned her long black hair and let it drape around her shoulders like a shawl.

I find a throne made of stones, sit down, and lean back. It feels delicious to lean back like this, without a sling to stop me.

I begin to dream with my eyes wide open about what life might be like here in this new country.

I hope there will be a house, of course, with some nice things inside. A real crib for Rose. Beds with soft mattresses. Quilts—the blue and yellow ones and new ones that I've made myself. Chairs, including one with rockers. A table covered with blue-and-white dishes. A vase in the middle of the table for flowers. And I want shelves, too.

With books.

Rose can help me in the house and in our garden, but I will give her plenty of time to play. I can make her dolls from hollyhocks, the way I have seen little girls make them as we travel. Perhaps Papa and I can even buy her a doll with a china head. I want the doll's cheeks to be very, very pink.

And one day Rose will go to school.

All these pictures make me smile, and I think how funny it is that just a few days ago I was wishing for a life without Rose. That was before I went to the river with John and returned to find her missing.

Another picture flashes into my head: Brother Owen asking me for his baby back. I can see every single detail.

Brother Owen approaching me with his hat in his hand. Brother Owen thanking me. Brother Owen wanting to take Rose into his own arms so that he can be a proper father to his daughter. Brother Owen taking her off to their new home.

Even though the day is warm and bright, the air around me grows dark, as though the sun has slipped behind a cloud. My hands turn cold. A hot wind starts to blow, kicking up red dirt in my eyes, and I miss the feel of Rose upon my back.

I hurry back down the hillside to find her.

But not until I leave a prayer there on the altar of the mountain like old Abraham himself.

Dear God. Do not take my Rose away from me.

Thursday, September 4, 1856

❧

WEST OF FORT LARAMIE, WYOMING

"But why would she betray him? I don't understand her at all!"

I shout this to Catherine Jones over the top of her handcart. She's pulling, I'm pushing. Papa told me to help Catherine Jones because the trail is nothing but thick black mud today and everybody's wheels are getting stuck. It's rained for three days straight, and I'm soaked to the bloody, bloody bone. The night I saw the White Lady was the last night of good weather.

"She was in love with her Sir Lancelot," Catherine shouts, turning back toward me through the rain. She has a little smile on her lips. I amuse her, for some reason.

"Yes, I know," I shout back, carefully lifting my feet so

I won't lose my shoes, "but she was married to King Arthur. Did she forget she already had a husband?"

Catherine Jones has been telling me stories to help pass the time. She reads them, then carries them in her head. Who would have suspected that such a silent person could have a treasure chest so full of precious words? Catherine Jones knows poems, too, long ones about doomed lovers. She also knows about history and languages, as well as everything there is to know about plants.

She'll bend over, pluck up a plant by its roots as though it were misbehaving, and say, "Boil this to its marrow and you'll have a nice blue dye." One day she showed me a plant for soothing burns. And then she touched her rough scar.

The other night Sister Bowen told me and Papa that Catherine Jones has decided to go to Ogden with us, and I am glad of it. Some days she travels with me and Papa and Rose. Her stories can almost make us forget how hard our trek has become since crossing the border into Wyoming, where the trail is full of gravel that chews up our feet and our wheels.

The other problem is that all of us in the company are running very low on supplies. I'm constantly weak. Lightheaded. At night in the tent you can hear stomachs rumble like thunder in hollow caves. The other day I found little George Jenkins sucking on a leather strap. It hurt my heart to watch his tiny lips work.

I heard Papa and Brother Bowen talking things over last night.

"Can we hold out?" Papa was saying, his voice grave.

"What choice is there?" Brother Bowen answered. "Our Captain Bunker must be either a saint or a fool to make this trip again for the likes of us."

Today in the pouring rain Catherine Jones has been telling me stories about King Arthur, who lived in a castle called Tintagel near the English border. He was Welsh like us, although the English say he was one of them. That's how the English are. Always taking credit for things they have no right to take credit for.

Anyway, I like King Arthur. He sounds like Papa. But Queen Guinevere! She broke King Arthur's heart.

"I hate Guinevere," I shout at Catherine.

Catherine just shrugs. "Maybe you'll understand her better one day when you are a woman, Charlotte."

"No, I won't," I say, stung that Catherine does not think I am a woman yet in spite of my secret breasts.

One thing I know about myself is that I am very loyal. When I give my heart to someone, I will give it forever. Not like Queen Guinevere.

Rose whimpers on my back. Poor little flower. She must be drenched. But what can I do other than to keep her head covered with a soggy corner of blanket?

Just ahead, Papa slows down, and so do we.

"The company is halting," he calls back to us, the rain

rolling off his poor bare head. "Maybe a cow's loose again."

Catherine mumbles something about there being nothing as stupid or as stubborn in this world as a cow. Unless it's a man.

"For the love of heaven, stop treading on my toes, Husband!"

It's Ellenor and Elias Lewis, coming up behind us. I turn just in time to see Ellenor punch her husband hard in the arm. Both of them look surprised by what has just passed between them. Then Ellenor throws her arms around his neck and bursts into tears, while Elias holds her tight.

Rose whimpering.

Catherine Jones muttering.

Ellenor punching.

A woman's scream shreds the soggy air. Catherine and I look at each other.

Another scream.

Catherine and I secure her handcart. Papa does the same. Then we run in the direction of the noise.

A small crowd clusters by the side of the trail. The Bowens. The Robertses. Others. As I race toward them, Rose bouncing upon my back, I see that their faces are white and grim. A man breaks loose from the little group, staggers toward a small clump of bushes, and vomits there.

It's Rose's father, Thomas Owen.

Papa joins Brother Owen and lays a hand across his back for support. "Steady, Thomas."

Brother Owen is still doubled over, losing what little bit is left in his stomach. The noise of his retching fills my ears, and I keep my distance. I don't want him to see Rose.

He'd better forget all about Rose.

After a moment, Brother Owen straightens up and runs his ragged sleeve across his mouth. His hair is wild and his brown eyes are dazed. He moans and takes Papa by the shirt.

I step back even farther.

"Tell me, Daniel," Brother Owen says. "Did we bury my Mary deep?"

Papa blinks. "Well, yes. We did. I'm sure of it, Thomas."

Brother Owen's voice sounds like a cross between the cry of a man and the growl of an animal. "Don't lie to me, Daniel Edwards."

Papa's own voice is low and calm. "I wouldn't do that. As you well know."

Brother Owen releases his grip, finger by finger, and smooths out the brand-new wrinkles on Papa's shirt. "I do know. Forgive me."

Papa slides an arm across Brother Owen's shoulder. But first he steals a glance at the group a short distance away. I know what Papa is thinking: *What did Brother Owen see over there on the side of the trail that upset him so?*

Whatever it is, I would like to see it for myself.

I turn and walk toward the group. Catherine is there already.

"No!" Brother Owen shouts after me. I turn to face him.

"Daniel, please tell her not to look," Brother Owen moans. "She's just a child."

First Catherine tells me I am not a woman. Now Brother Owens tells Papa I'm a child.

I shift the bundle on my back. I am more of a man than he is.

Papa looks at me and I throw out my chin.

"Our Charlotte is not such a little girl these days," says Papa.

He gives me a slight nod. A nod that says I am free to do what I choose to do.

And what I want to do is see. Good things. Evil things. All things.

I turn my back on Thomas Owen, not caring whether he sees Rose this time. In fact, I'm happy to flaunt Rose in his face. He does not deserve her.

"What is it?" I ask the group.

I can feel Catherine's strange eyes on my face as I step forward to look.

At first, all I see are little mounds of soggy black earth, as though some dog has been digging for bones. And then I see the rest.

It is the dress I think I will remember each night as I

wander through the landscape of my dreams. Dark blue like the sky right before nightfall. Little white buttons scattered down the front like stars. I know that if I pulled that torn stained dress over my head right now, it would fit me. Perfectly.

This girl was someone my own age.

"Wolves," someone whispers.

"Her people didn't bury her body deep enough, poor sweet girl," another says. "The wolves dug her up."

"God rest her soul," Sister Bowen breathes.

I slide my hand behind my waist until I can feel Rose's tiny balled-up foot. Oh, I am so glad that my little girl baby cannot see or understand this terrible thing at our feet.

"Come," says Brother Bowen, "let's do right by our sister here. Shovels."

And so we dig another grave for this nameless daughter and sister who will never be a mother. We sing her songs and bid her farewell, although we do not know her name.

Brother Bowen speaks for each of us. " 'When I was a child, I spake as a child, I understood as a child, I thought as a child: but when I became a man, I put away childish things. For now we see through a glass, darkly.' "

When the time comes, I throw great handfuls of dirt on the grave, while Papa sits in the distance with Thomas Owen, holding him in his arms.

It's cold in our tent tonight. My breath hangs like a little white cloud in the air. I'm holding Rose hard to my heart this sleepless night so she'll be warm as I sing soft into her thick, thick hair.

"*The Mormons were camped down by the green
    grove
Where the clear waters flow from the mountains
    above.
The wind it approached, all chilly and cold,
And we listened to the howling of those lonesome
    roving wolves.*

"*The groans of the dying were heard in our camp,
And the cold chilly frost, it was seen on our tent,
And the fear in our hearts can never be told
As we listened to the howling of those lonesome
    roving wolves.*

"*The grave of the stranger we left on the plain
Down by the green grove, there forever to remain.
To remember his grave we left ashes and coals
To hide him from the savages and the lonesome
    roving wolves.*

"*But early next morning, just at the break of day,
The drums and the fifes did play our reveille.
Our mules were brought in, our baggage for to pull,*

*And now we'll bid adieu to those lonesome
    roving wolves."*

Rose's little hand crawls up my neck. Her nails scratch my skin. I must find a way to trim them tomorrow. I take her hand, pull it up to my mouth, and kiss each finger. One by one by one.

I will never sing this song again.

Thursday, September 11, 1856

❧

OUTSIDE CASPER, WYOMING

I believe I could bear the rest—the pushing, the pulling, the cold, the feel of rocks beneath my feet, the weight of Rose upon my back, the crowded tent at night, the smells of other people, the way Brother Roberts's right eye twitches when he hooks you with a look, the way Sister Bowen snores but says she doesn't—I could stand all this if I weren't starving.

What I would give to fill my stomach this afternoon!

Right now I'm trying to make me and Papa our midday meal. Flour. Sugar. Coffee. Almost all gone. I might as well make our meal out of air. Papa shares what little food we have left, though. So does everyone else.

Except, of course, for the most righteous Brother and Sister Roberts.

"Why don't they share like the rest of us?" I asked Papa one night as he rocked Rose in the starlight.

"Because they're afraid," he said.

Afraid? Well. I'm afraid, too. Afraid that we will all run out of supplies and drop along the trail like scrawny stiff dead birds before we reach Fort Bridger.

Rose lies on Mam's yellow quilt, shielded from the sun, which is bright, although the air is cool. She starts to fuss but thinks better of it. Instead she pops her middle two fingers into her mouth.

I cannot stand that my Rose has to comfort herself this way because her stomach is empty in spite of Rosa Jenkins's milk. A baby, at least, shouldn't have to be hungry.

There is the rumble of horse thunder in the distance. I know this sound. Indians.

I look up, squint, see them coming. They wear rich flowing robes stitched out of the skins of many animals. Their long hair is the color of ravens, and the manes of their sweating horses stream behind them in the wind like wings in motion.

My knees go weak. My eyes fill with tears. These Indians look like screaming angels descending upon our camp. Angels coming to save us all.

We trade what we can. I give them Mam's flax blue

quilt. I rub it against my cheek before handing it over in exchange for a little bag of flour—smooth white gold. The brave takes the rolled quilt and tucks it beneath his arm, satisfied. Papa digs into his pocket, removes a balled-up piece of cloth, opens it, and reveals a garnet ring. The one we traded for weeks ago.

The one Papa said might save us someday.

The brave picks up the ring, looks at it carefully, and smiles. He gives Papa sugar and dried meat because he is generous and pleased with this gift. The man touches Rose's hair before he leaves, and I think his touch is a blessing that will keep Rose safe from wolves.

Almost as quickly as they came, they are gone, their cries filling the air around us.

Sister Roberts walks past me. Her face is pinched and white, and she clutches a sack of something in her right hand.

Her cameo is gone.

Saturday, September 20, 1856

❧

NORTHEAST OF FORT BRIDGER, WYOMING

"*I'm King John of America!*"

He's standing on a rock in a river, roaring at an osprey making lazy circles overhead. I'm standing in the water nearby, laughing, and I am beautiful enough to break your heart. My hair is gold and my skin is the color of cream. Around my ankles, tiny green and purple and red fish flash in the sun-lit water. I could scoop up these strange fish in my arms and wear them in my hair and on my arms and hands like jewels.

It's summer again.

One whimper and I'm wide awake. Rose is ready for her early-morning breakfast. I lie still, keeping my eyes closed a minute longer. No use. The dream and all its colors have faded.

Rose cries again. Papa stirs.

At first I'm annoyed with Rose. I hardly dream now because Rose wakes me so often during the night. But she's a baby, after all. Papa says I woke up him and Mam all night long.

"She's a much better baby than you ever were," Papa always tells me with a grin.

I roll over and trail a finger down her cheek, distressed to find that her skin is so cold. "You'll feel better soon, love. I promise."

I bundle Rose into my arms and pick my way over sleeping bodies to the corner where Rosa, George, and Emma Jenkins make their beds each night. Along the way I nearly step on John's head. His dark hair lies unruly on his blanket, and his mouth is slightly open. He snores. Like his mother.

I smile. Truly, he's still King John of America. Even when he's catching flies with that mouth as he sleeps.

"Sister Jenkins," I whisper to a mound of untidy blankets and shawls. "Rose is hungry."

There is no sound. No movement.

"Sister Jenkins?"

No response at all. Not even the sound of breathing.

I bend over and touch Rosa Jenkins. Only, she isn't here. Neither are Emma and George.

I stand up and blink. It's night. It's cold. Where can they be?

Rose is starting to shove her fist into her mouth and suck. She needs Sister Jenkins. I sway back and forth with her in my arms, whispering to her, so that my hair spills into her face and she grabs it with her free hand. This works for now. But soon my Rose will be screaming.

I must find Sister Jenkins.

I pick my way back over bodies like a horse down a mountain trail. I take Mam's yellow quilt off the tent floor and throw it like a cape around my shoulders. Then Rose and I go outside.

The thin mountain air, so different from the heavy prairie air, slaps me cold in the face. I hold Rose close to my chest and make sure the blanket covers her, especially her ears. Sister Bowen has taught me how to do this so that Rose won't have earaches.

The sound of muffled coughing from other tents echoes throughout the camp. So many in the company are ill these days! I look up at the white stars above and mutter a hasty prayer.

Please, God, please. Spare Rose.

A mouse scampers across the ground and into the bushes. An owl, looking for some breakfast of his own, hoots with interest. I wait for my own eyes to grow large just like an owl's so that I can find Sister Jenkins and her children.

Rose and I go roving through the camp.

Where is she? In another tent with friends? I snort

out loud. Sister Jenkins barely speaks these days—just plods along mute while John and Morgan and the other boys take turns helping her with her handcart. There are no friends.

Rose has started rooting against my chest, looking for something there to eat. Her body grows tense.

Think, Charlotte! Think!

Something is very wrong.

A wind kicks up and swirls the hem of my blanket. My wild hair falls into my face. I chew on my lip, thinking. Then I race back to our tent and crouch next to Papa.

"Papa! Wake up!" I grab his shoulder and shake hard.

His eyelids flutter with fatigue.

"Something has happened to Sister Jenkins and the babies."

Now Papa's eyes focus on my face. I tell him of the blankets with no one under them.

Papa sits straight up now. I watch his face change into something hard and grim while I finish my story. He gets up and wakes Brother Bowen.

"Rosa and her children have gone missing, James," Papa says. "They left all their blankets here."

Brother Bowen tosses off his own blanket with a single violent motion. "On a cruel night such as this? Come, Daniel. We must inform the sentinels immediately and form a search party."

In less time than I would have thought possible, a

group of men, including John, is fanning out from the campsite to comb the surrounding area.

Those of us who stay behind build a fire and pray for the safe deliverance of Rosa and her children. As I bow my head, I see something out of the corner of my eye.

The White Lady. Looking ahead to the next day's journey.

Rose, worn out with hunger, falls fast asleep in my arms. I leave the group by the fire and take my baby to the tent so she can sleep where it is quiet. As I lift a blanket to drape over her, my blood freezes. There is a snake sleeping at the bottom of Papa's bedroll.

The sound of my racing heart must fill the whole tent. But I reach for the little knife I always keep with me. Just that quick, I strike. Warm blood hits my hand.

Rose will not have to worry about snakes this morning.

And I am glad that I have such skill as a player of mumblety-peg.

The search party does not return until the sun has risen. John carries George, wrapped up tight in a blanket. Elias Lewis holds Emma, who makes more noise than one baby girl should, although her sounds make all of us around the fire smile with relief. Papa leads Sister Jenkins by the hand. Her pale hair tumbles around her boney shoulders. She looks frail, lost like that poor silvery woman in Brother Bowen's ghost story. If someone were to ask her her own name right now, I'm sure she wouldn't recall it.

"Our lambs are found and returned safely to the fold," Brother Bowen says as though Rosa Jenkins and Emma and George had all wandered off by mistake sometime during the middle of the night.

I look at the faces of the children sitting around the campfire—little Mary and Hyrum and Jacob—and I think of the far-off day we found beads together in the anthill.

Perhaps it's just as well for them to believe that the evening's events have only been some terrible accident. That is what I would want Rose to think if she were their age.

As a log pops and embers spray and the scent of woodsmoke braids itself into my hair, I cannot help re-membering the words Mam made me memorize from the Bible.

Now the serpent was more subtil than any beast of the field which the Lord God had made. And he said unto the woman, "Yea, hath God said, 'Ye shall not eat of every tree of the garden'?"

And the woman said unto the serpent, "We may eat of the fruit of the trees of the garden:

"But of the fruit of the tree which is in the midst of the garden, God hath said, 'Ye shall not eat of it, neither shall ye touch it, lest ye die.'"

And the serpent said unto the woman, "Ye shall not surely die:

"For God doth know that in the day ye eat thereof, then your eyes shall be opened, and ye shall be as gods, knowing good and evil."

Good and evil. Evil and good. My eyes have seen what they have seen. Rosa Jenkins meant to die last night.

Sister Bowen stands and walks toward Rosa Jenkins. So does Sister Roberts. They flank Rosa Jenkins as they adjust the blanket that slips from her shoulders and push back the hair that spills into her vacant eyes.

Sister Roberts shoots Elias and John hot looks.

"Take care of Emma and George while Margaret and I see to Rosa," she orders.

John shifts George, who throws back his head and laughs.

For the first time in a long time, Rosa and George have hot bread for supper. I can see them both right now, breaking it apart with their fingers as steam rises from the doughy center.

Who has shared their bread with them this evening?

I wish it had been me.

Monday, September 22, 1856

❧

NEAR FORT BRIDGER, WYOMING

The sun this morning was pink and amber—just like the inside of a seashell. It climbed a perfect cloudless sky and drenched the trail with its light. After days of cold, the air above and the earth below hum with warmth.

"A fine autumn day like this is a gift," Sister Bowen said as she folded the last of her quilts and strapped them onto the handcart.

Later, as we walked, Ellenor kept whooping like a wild Indian girl. She hiked up her shabby skirts, which have frayed up to her ankles, and did a jig. Elias laughed each time she did it. Once he even stopped pulling the handcart and clapped a little tune for her.

I hope that when I marry, my husband and I will love each other as much as Elias and Ellenor do. I hope that he will give me love spoons that he has carved with his own two hands.

The rest of the company sang for the first time in many days as they pulled their possessions. We're happy to be so close to Fort Bridger, where we can get the supplies we'll need for the rest of our journey.

It felt wonderful to sing again. Music is air if you're Welsh.

> *"High on the mountaintop*
> *A banner is unfurled.*
> *Ye nations, now look up;*
> *It waves to all the world.*
> *In Deseret's sweet, peaceful land—*
> *On Zion's mount behold it stand!"*

Voices chased one another along the trail like kittens. Brother Bowen's booming off-key voice. Elizabeth the Musical's clear high voice. Papa's perfect tenor voice. Even Brother and Sister Roberts sang. And so did Rosa Jenkins, in a weak sputtering voice.

She tried.

The only person who didn't sing was Catherine Jones. But then, Catherine never does anything just because the rest of us are doing it.

"Charlotte," Catherine said when we stopped for our noonday meal, "let me take your Rose so that you and John can sit together in that grove over there."

So John and I ate together, surrounded by slim tall tree soldiers. Western trees, Captain Bunker says. Aspens. The branches were loaded with leaves that looked like bright yellow coins. They jingled and shook against a bright blue sky. If I could fill my arms with those branches, I would be as rich as Queen Victoria.

John bit into his bread angrily. "I don't understand it, Charlotte," he finally said when his meal was finished.

I looked at him and wanted to touch his jaw with my fingers. "Understand what?"

"Wanting to die." He picked up a stone and threw it hard. A squirrel scolded him, then raced up a tree trunk. "Wanting your children to die."

I didn't say anything because I was too busy imagining Sister Jenkins gathering up her babies and stealing away in the middle of the night.

I cannot imagine doing that to my Rose.

John picked up another stone and threw that one, too. His face was grim. "Mam told me not to judge Sister Jenkins too harshly. She said some people can't bear the burden of their sorrows."

He flung another stone. "Maybe my mam wouldn't be so forgiving if she were the one who'd found those babies."

"Was it bad?" I asked in a soft voice.

"Yes," whispered John. "When I go to sleep from now on, I'll hear them cry."

A noise. Quick as animals, John and I turned to look behind us. It was an antelope—all lean and velvet brown. She watched us for a minute. Held us with her strange dark eyes. And then she leapt away like a dancer deep into the aspens around us.

And so I think as I kiss my Rose's fingers and rock her to sleep beneath the night sky that in many ways it was a perfect day. Bright sun. Blue sky. Songs. John. Only two things happened that unsettled me.

First thing. When John and I joined Catherine Jones after eating our meal, Catherine told me that she'd had a visitor.

"Who?" I asked.

"Thomas Owen," she said in a low even voice. I had the feeling Catherine was watching me closely to see how I would react.

"What did he want?"

"To ask after Rose."

I laughed this away. But a cold tiny finger touched my heart.

Second thing. Rose has started to cough.

Monday, September 29, 1856

❧

Near Echo Canyon, Utah

"The meeting starts in five minutes," says Brother Bowen. "I'm told that Captain Bunker has a special announcement for all of us tonight."

He claps Papa on the back. "Hurry up. You know how the captain hates stragglers."

I lick my fingers and slick down the front of Rose's hair. Her forehead is hot. "What do you think Captain Bunker wants to tell us?"

Papa shrugs. "I don't know. But James is certainly in a merry mood, so it must be good news."

I would relish hearing some good news.

Rose's cough has grown worse. She was limp with exhaustion against my back today as we wound our way over steep mountain trails. This made her even heavier to carry. Strange how a tired, sick baby weighs more than a lively baby flapping her arms.

I glance at Rose nestled in my arms. Her cheeks flame like tiny pink flowers.

Sister Bowen and Catherine have told me to keep her warm and feed her teaspoons of water. Which I have done now for three days.

"Shall we join the others, Charlotte?" Papa smiles at me, and I follow him to the clearing where all three hundred members of our company assemble.

The meeting is called to order. One of the brothers says an opening prayer. We sing. Then Captain Bunker stands before us, his battered hat in his lean hands. A campfire blazes behind him, so that he looks huge against a halo of light.

Papa and I sit on the edge of the group, near the front. Catherine Jones joins us.

"Brothers and Sisters, it pleases me greatly to tell you that the day of our deliverance is at hand. Like the Children of Israel preparing to enter the Promised Land, we will reach the valley of the Great Salt Lake in a few days' time."

Applause erupts like a clap of thunder. A wide smile stretches across the captain's brown face.

"It has been my great honor to serve as your leader."

Oh! I can understand much of what he says before Brother Roberts translates!

"This has been a long trek, hard and sometimes dangerous," Captain Bunker continues. "And the most difficult part of the trail is to come. Big Mountain. Little Mountain. Emigration Canyon. But you will prevail, just as you have prevailed for all these months.

"When we began this journey, you knew nothing of life on the trail. You were miners and factory workers, seamstresses and housemaids. But you learned. And you endured with uncommon courage. You are rich in strength and belief. You make me proud to call myself a Mormon man."

A mighty cheer leaps up from the crowd. I look at Papa and see that there are tears trapped and sparkling in his red beard. Then he lifts both arms over his head and begins to shout with happiness. Catherine watches him beneath the shadow of her dark hair, smiling.

And now there's music. Fiddling. People young and old jump to their feet and dance beneath these hard stars.

Papa reaches across me and Rose to take Catherine by the hand.

She opens her mouth but does not say anything as Papa helps her to her feet and leads her to a clearing where everyone is dancing.

I watch Papa and Catherine dance together as I sit on a nearby log and rock my Rose. Catherine is graceful, but truly Papa is as clumsy as one of the company's cows.

I did not realize until now that Papa dances very badly. I almost feel sorry for him.

John joins me. "Sister Jones looks beautiful tonight, doesn't she?"

"Yes." It's funny how seldom I notice her scar now.

John looks at Rose sleeping in my arms. Her breath is shallow and fast, like the panting of a pup. "How is she tonight, Charlotte?"

I sigh. "No better than she was last night, even though I'm doing everything I know how to make her better."

John touches her tiny button of a nose. "I know you are," he says.

Catherine breaks away from Papa and joins us. "Give me Rose, Charlotte," she orders in a gruff voice. "It's your turn to dance with him."

Then Catherine blushes.

So I dance with Papa, who does not, for some reason, stomp on my feet the way he was stepping all over Catherine Jones's toes.

I dance with Brother Bowen.

I dance with John and Morgan and the two little boys, Hyrum and Jacob, who discovered beads with me that day along the trail. I even dance with little Mary, who wears a necklace made from the beads we collected together.

But I'm not prepared for the person who taps my shoulder next.

He takes off his hat, sweeps me a bow, then leads me in a dance.

I am dancing with Captain Edward Bunker!

"You're the girl who has carried the Owens' baby all this way, aren't you?" he says.

I nod.

He doesn't say more, but what he has said is enough.

I feel bold. "May I ask you a question, Captain Bunker?" I say in broken English.

"Of course."

"Are there fireflies in Utah?"

Captain Bunker laughs. "No."

"I will miss the fireflies," I say, remembering the way they lit up our hot prairie nights.

"Step outside one summer evening as the sun sets and watch the mountains around the Salt Lake valley turn blue," says Captain Bunker. "I promise you won't miss your fireflies once you've seen Zion's hills at twilight."

Blue mountains beneath a blue sky beneath a blue heaven.

I cannot wait.

Oh, I am dancing still!

My feet remember every step they took with Captain Bunker. My arms tingle with music. I spin around and around and around beneath these dark trees while my hair swirls around me.

Ahead, a group of women are clustered by a dying fire. Catherine is with them, Rose tucked tight in her arms. Even from this distance, I can see that she is still.

Good. My baby is sleeping.

I smile as I walk toward the women—Catherine, Sister Bowen, Ellenor, Sister Jenkins. I even smile at Sister Roberts. Their faces are reflected in the firelight. Shadows leap across their skin. No one smiles back.

I lift my skirts and race toward them.

"What's wrong?" I hover over Rose and see that a pink moon of color burns on each cheek.

"Her fever is worse," says Sister Bowen. "Much worse."

I begin to quake. "What can I do to help her?"

The sisters shift in their seats. Ellenor looks down at her feet.

"Tell me what to do!"

"Charlotte, let me care for Rose tonight. I have some experience in these matters." Catherine's voice is low, as if she is prepring to beguile me with her stories. Only I won't listen to her. Not tonight.

"No, Catherine!" I stomp toward her and thrust out my arms. "Give her to me. Now."

Catherine and Sister Bowen trade glances. Then Catherine stands and slips Rose into my arms. Oh, this baby is hot! Terrible, terrible hot.

But I will make her better.

"We'll all take turns helping you with our Rose baby tonight," says Sister Bowen.

There are murmurs of agreement. I give a quick nod to show thanks. "She will get better, won't she?"

Sister Bowen picks through the folds of her skirt for a minute before looking at me straight. "I'll be honest, since you deserve the truth, Charlotte. You've taken care of her in every way, but a violent fever in a baby so young is a very dangerous thing. We will do what we can for her and pray for the rest."

Pray for the rest?

What does Sister Bowen mean? Does she think this baby girl lying limp in my arms will not get better? How dare she! How dare any of these women—these *faithful, God-fearing sisters*—think that my Rose might die after God himself spared her life at birth.

It will not be.

Tears spring to my eyes, but my voice is sure. "We don't need your help. Rose will live."

Seconds pass like minutes. Minutes pass like hours. Hours stretch into endless night. Outside the wind moans. Inside Rose coughs her breath away. She is too weak to cry. Too weak to fight.

Oh, Rose. My poor baby.

I do all the things I have been told to do. Keep her warm. Give her water. Place a damp rag upon her head.

"Fear not," the angels said. But I am afraid. Truly.

All night long the women take turns sitting by me. Each one tells me to use her first name. Ellenor. Rosa. Lititia. Margaret. They sing us lullabies. They pray over us. They braid and unbraid my thick hair with swift gentle hands.

"Please sleep, dear girl," Margaret whispers in my ear. "Let me hold Rose while you sleep."

But I will not let her take my Rose.

When Catherine sits next to me, Rose pants harder, as though she cannot fill her tiny lungs with enough air.

I pull her tight to my chest. Tighter and tighter.

What's happening to her now? I do not understand.

Catherine hums the tune of an old song. It's familiar. Did Mam sing it to me? I can't remember. I can't remember. . . .

There are so many things I cannot remember.

The inside of the tent begins to grow brighter, as though the moon has come for a visit. I look around, surprised by how clearly I can see everyone as they sleep. Or don't sleep. Rosa Jenkins lies on her bedroll, stroking little George's hair and watching me closely.

"Why is it so light in here?" I whisper to Catherine.

She squints. "Light?"

I look at her. Is she teasing me? Can't she see the light for herself?

"It's as though there's a window in the ceiling," I explain. "And the stars are as bright as the sun."

Catherine presses her palm against my forehead. "Charlotte. Dearest love. Listen to me. You *must* let me take Rose now. I will watch over her while you sleep."

Her voice is urgent. She thinks I have Rose's fever, too. But I'm not ill. There's light here. Light—

Oh! I understand it now.

The White Lady.

She's just outside the tent, looking ahead to the next day's journey. A journey that this Rose and I will make together.

I laugh out loud. Catherine places her hand on my shoulder, but I shake her away! All is well! All is well! My baby and I have not been forgotten!

Rose rattles in my arms. She draws a tiny ragged breath. And then. Then she is still.

"Rose?" I whisper. "Rose!"

Catherine holds her hand above Rose's nose and mouth. "She has stopped breathing."

"No!"

Catherine tries to take her from me, but I cling to Rose. My Rose. I fold her up in my arms and will not allow another soul to touch her.

I bring her cheek next to my cheek, and I sing to her with hot words.

> *"You're going to a new place,*
> *a safe place,*
> *a place for you to play*
> *and a place for you to grow,*
> *a place where you will tend your house*
> *and your garden dressed with Rose—"*

"Charlotte, Charlotte," Catherine pleads.

I ignore her. I ignore the others who begin to crowd around me in the tent. Sweat covers me like another skin. Rose's hair grows damp. Outside I can hear the beating of a bird's wings. I sing to the rhythm of those wings.

> *You're going to a new place,*
> *a safe place. . . .*
> *You're going to a new place,*
> *a safe place. . . ."*

Over and over I sing Rose's song.

> *"You're going to a new place—"*

Rose shudders. She takes a breath. The noise of the wings stops. The light inside the tent fades.

I cling to Rose and bathe her face with my tears.

It's a miracle, everyone says the next morning as they break down the tents and load their handcarts for the last leg of our trek. A true latter-day miracle! The baby Rose's fever broke in the early hours of the morning. She is weak, they all say, but alive. Thanks to Charlotte.

The White Lady.

Who was she? I wonder as Papa watches me to make sure I sip the weak herb tea Catherine has brewed for me. A ghost? An angel?

My mam? Rose's mam?

Or was she someone I invented? A character in one of my stories?

I don't know who she was. Or what she was. But I do know this:

I will never see her again.

Tuesday, September 30, 1856

❧

Echo Canyon, Utah

I sing one of Catherine's lullabies to Rose, who smiles up at me.

I cannot believe that our long, long walk is almost over. We enter the Promised Valley in two days' time!

Papa grins as he lashes the last of the cooking utensils to the handcart. "Someone's happy this morning."

Rose flaps her arms, and I laugh.

"What do you think Salt Lake City looks like, Papa?"

"I've heard the streets are clean and wide."

"Not like the streets in Port Talbot."

He chuckles. "No."

"Excuse me, Brother Edwards. Charlotte."

My blood grows cold as I turn to face Brother

Thomas Owen. I've felt his dark eyes upon Rose and me ever since the day we found the body of the girl alongside the trail. And his interest in us has been even keener since the night Rose nearly died.

He clears his throat. Shifts his weight from one leg to the other. Fiddles with the hat in his hands. "I want to speak to you both."

He gives us a little smile, which I don't return.

"Thomas!" Papa says with a grin. "How are you?"

Brother Owen hesitates. "I am . . . well."

"Truly?" asks Papa.

"Truly," he says. And he sounds sure of himself this time. "A black cloud has lifted these past few days. I am nearly myself again."

"We are pleased to hear you say so, Thomas," says Papa.

Speak for yourself, I say to Papa in my head.

"Thank you, Daniel," says Brother Owen. "I owe both of you a debt of gratitude."

Brother Owen looks straight at me and I take a step back. Dread fills my bones.

"You saved my daughter's life the other night," says Brother Owen.

I pull Rose closer.

"Thank you, Charlotte."

I shrug.

"When I heard that my baby nearly died, it was as though God himself took me by the shoulders and shook me. What if my daughter died and I didn't know her? That would be a terrible thing."

Papa nods.

Brother Owen smiles at me. How could I ever have thought he was handsome that night on the ship when I made him a prince?

He fiddles some more with his stupid hat. "Thank you, Charlotte, for caring for my daughter all along. At first I was barely aware of what you were doing. I was too absorbed by my own selfish grief. But now I know full well what you've done. For the baby. Me. Mary."

I'm holding my Rose so tight, she starts to cry. Brother Owen reaches to comfort her, but I shrink from him.

His hand drops and his face changes as he looks at me. Perhaps he begins to understand how much I despise him.

"I don't know what came over me to neglect my duties as I have done," he says, shaking his head. "Mary must be so ashamed of the way I have behaved. I am ashamed of myself."

Papa rests an easy hand on Brother Owen's shoulder. "Look at me, Thomas."

Papa and Brother Owen turn to each other. "We all have our evil seasons," says Papa in a low voice. And then they embrace.

"Thank you," whispers Brother Owen into the collar of Papa's shirt. He swallows hard when he finally pulls himself away from Papa. Stands up straight. Opens his mouth to say something but waits until his words are clear.

"I am here this morning to do the thing that should have been done before. I am here to claim my child, to take care of her and to love her as you, Brother Daniel Edwards, have always taken care of your Charlotte. I pray to God that I can be as good a father as you have been, Daniel. And I pray my daughter may grow to be as strong and as beautiful a woman as your daughter."

I tremble and cannot breathe.

"*You!*" I say through my teeth to Brother Owen. "You gave her up. You cannot have her back!"

Rose is screaming now. I shove her head into my shoulder to stifle her noise. Then I turn and run away so fast and so far that the camp becomes a blur behind me.

Nobody scolds me when I return, even though it's clear we're getting a late start because of me. In fact, nobody says anything, although I do catch some of them staring at me, their eyes full of questions.

Which I ignore.

So I pretend that nothing has changed. Things are just the way they've been for many mornings now. Papa pulling. Me pushing. Rose riding high up on my back. Except that maybe I am talking more than usual, like a blue jay sitting on the limb of a pine tree.

"You'll have a new white dress for your eighth birthday, Rose," I tell her. "I'll make it for you myself. And I'll braid your long black princess hair into a crown the day you're baptized."

Papa lets out a groan as he pulls the cart over a cropping of stone.

"Charlotte," he puffs, "Rose will always be in our hearts. But she doesn't belong to us. She belongs with her father."

Her father? Who will live so far away he might as well be dead to us?

"You're wrong," I say. Then I sing loudly enough to drown out his voice and the voices in my head.

> *"And maidens fair will dance and sing,*
> *Young men more happy than a king,*
> *And children too will laugh and play;*
> *Their strength increasing day by day."*

Oh, you are wrong.

Wednesday, October 1, 1856

❧

EAST CANYON, UTAH

"I can take her for you now if you would like, Charlotte."

Sister Rosa Jenkins stands in front of me as I finish changing Rose before I prepare our noonday meal. George and Emma (who has just started to walk this week!) peek out at me from behind her tattered skirts.

"Rose is fine, Sister Jenkins. Thank you."

Rose looks up from Mam's yellow quilt and smiles. When she first started smiling, she smiled at everyone who came into view. But now that she is almost three months old, Rose is picky. Most of her smiles are for me.

Sister Jenkins nods, then leaves with George and

Emma trailing behind her, kicking up little clouds of trail dust.

Truly I believe Sister Jenkins offered to help so she could hear for herself the true story of how Charlotte said no.

Thomas Owen wanted his baby girl back yesterday, and Charlotte Edwards said no.

I have heard those words whispered more than once since yesterday. Meanwhile, people stroll by our handcart and say hello to Papa, but it is me and Rose they stare at.

Stare all you like.

Papa grunts as he runs his hand over the wheel he is repairing.

"Daniel! Charlotte!" Brother Bowen sings out a greeting as he approaches us. John is at his side.

Papa and Brother Bowen speak of practical things— where we will all stay when we arrive in the valley tomorrow—but their eyes drift toward me.

John, on the other hand, looks at me straight on, his arms folded across his chest. There is a challenge in his face. So finally I look back at him without flinching, even though my heart is pounding.

"Let's talk," he says.

I don't answer.

He grabs my arm and pulls me to my feet. He will not let go of me, even though I try to slip from his grasp.

"Charlotte and I are going for a walk," he announces to our fathers. His voice is grim.

Papa and Brother Bowen trade glances and nod.

Rose cries. Papa picks her up, but she doesn't stop.

"It sounds as if she still has some bubbles in her stomach," I say. Papa rubs her back. Rose keeps crying.

I shake myself free from John. I take Rose and heave her over my left shoulder. One hard pat and she belches more loudly than a boy showing off in front of friends.

"There," I say, handing Rose back to Papa. "She'll nap now."

John takes my arm again and pulls me away so that we are alone. I yank my arm free again, and the two of us square off like dogs over a bone.

"You have no right to drag me away like that," I snap.

"And you have no right to keep Rose," he snaps back. "She belongs with her father."

John's words come at me like a kick in the stomach. That he of all people is saying this to me! John should want the same thing I want.

"How is Brother Owen her father?" I shout so loudly that I startle two birds sitting on a branch overhead. "I cared for her, carried her, and cleaned her. I made sure she didn't starve. I watch over her when she goes to sleep and when she wakes up. I sing to her and tell her stories. I named her. And I am the one who loves her."

"You're not Rose's mother." John says this slowly, as

though he is speaking to a half-wit. "You're a thirteen-year-old girl."

A girl? A child? After all that I've done?

I slap him so hard my hand stings. John touches the side of his face and stares at me. He turns. And leaves.

I choose to sit apart from the others tonight while they talk and sing and make plans for our entrance into the valley tomorrow. I sit on a log and let Rose play with my fingers as she blows little bubbles from her mouth.

She's changed so much. Already I can barely remember her rough skin and newborn's milk eyes.

A twig snaps behind me. "May I join you?"

It's Catherine, carrying a book.

I don't say anything, but she sweeps up her skirts and sits beside me anyway. She places her book on her lap. I try not to look interested, but I wonder what this one's about.

A breeze hums through the tops of the trees. The hoot of an owl rings through the air. The scent of dirt and pine fills my nose. It's a smell I have come to love since climbing into these high mountains. Will I smell it in the city below?

I hope so.

"This is hard," Catherine says simply.

I pull Rose closer to my heart. At last I nod. It feels good to hear someone say that word, *hard*.

"Remember the night you offered to take Rose?" Catherine asks. She is smiling a little.

"Yes." The night that everything changed for me?

"Here's what I wrote about it," says Catherine, opening her book. Her journal.

" 'Charlotte surprised us all tonight by offering to care of Mary Owen's baby. I suspect she was just showing off. Charlotte is a very lively child with a violent imagination who likes people to notice her.' "

I shoot Catherine an evil look. She grins at me, then continues.

" 'I predict that Charlotte's enthusiasm for the project will wear off in a few days. Then it will be up to the rest of us women to take care of the newborn baby because men are completely useless in this respect. Most likely the burden will fall on Margaret Bowen, a solid soul who must sometimes wonder why she married a daydreaming radical.' "

Catherine snaps shut her wicked journal. "Look at me."

I face her, hoping she will see how very displeased I am with her right now.

"I was wrong about you, wasn't I?" Catherine says. "You've been a good mother to our Rose here after all."

I gasp.

"Say it, Charlotte," Catherine says.

"Yes. I've been a good mother. Mostly."

Catherine laughs when I say "mostly."

"Well, my dear. That's the best any of us can hope for."

I slide a little closer to Catherine and even think

about putting my head on her shoulder, although I don't. The only time Catherine has ever touched me is the night Rose almost died.

I start playing with Rose's black hair. She has more hair than poor Emma Jenkins, who is still bald even though she's a year old.

"You know what I'm afraid of?" I ask.

"You? Afraid of something? I don't believe it."

I pull a face at Catherine and she laughs. Rose makes sweet little gurgling noises in her throat.

"All right then, Mistress Charlotte, what are you afraid of?"

"That I'll forget Rose." My throat turns thick, and I whisper the rest. "Just like I'm forgetting my mam."

Catherine looks at me as she strokes the cover of her journal with her long fingers.

"Charlotte," she says, "tell me everything you remember about your mam tonight. And then in the first light of morning, I will take this journal and I will write her down."

She reaches toward me and lifts a strand of my hair, twisting it like flax between her fingers. "I can teach you to read and write for yourself soon if you like."

My heart lifts. Catherine will teach me to read. Catherine will show me how to preserve my words.

"Let's start with this," Catherine says. "Charlotte is a good mam because she had a good mam."

I nod. "It's true. She cared for me and told me stories,

and held me when it rained, because I was afraid of thunder." I laugh a little, embarrassed by the baby I used to be. "She just said it was Jesus hammering things in heaven, because Jesus used to be a carpenter. Once when a man in rags was teasing me, Mam went after him with a stick."

Catherine nods.

"And she was beautiful. Just like Mary Owen was beautiful. Mam had long black hair. She wore it up during the day, but at night she let it down and I would comb it for her. Papa combed it, too. Her eyes were brown."

"It doesn't surprise me that your mam was beautiful," Catherine says. "You're beautiful, Charlotte."

"Oh!" I blush in the dark.

Catherine laughs. "You should see yourself in a proper mirror, Charlotte. You've turned into a woman since this trip began. No wonder John can't stop looking at you."

I blush some more, but her words make me ripe with happiness.

"What else do you remember about your mam?"

"She loved to sing loud."

"Now, who does that remind me of?" Catherine is smiling in the dark.

"She liked riddles and jokes and ghost stories."

"Surprise!"

"She made it her business to know things. The names

of plants, just like you. She also knew the names of stars. Mam loved the night sky—especially the moon."

I pause to look at the stars whose names Mam knew.

"She loved the Book of Mormon even though she couldn't read. She memorized passages from it by making people repeat them over and over to her. She wanted me to memorize Scripture things, too, and sometimes I did. But mostly I wanted to make up my own words."

Catherine laughs.

"Mam had a wicked temper sometimes, like Captain Bunker," I say. "Once she threw a dish at Papa's head because he made her so angry. But I saw her kiss him later, and they were both laughing."

"Some husbands and wives are more fortunate than others," Catherine says. By the light of the stars, I see the smile slip from her face.

"She wanted to move to Utah," I say. "But she died. She left us. Papa and me."

Catherine looks at the journal in her lap and traces a pattern on its cover with her finger. "I left babies, too, Charlotte."

My mouth flies open.

"A boy and a girl," Catherine says. "They were both handsome."

I can barely speak, I'm so surprised. "Where are they?"

"In Wales. Swansea. With their father. Happy, I hope, and well."

"Their father?"

Catherine keeps tracing patterns on the cover of her journal. "My husband."

Catherine looks straight at me to see how I am taking this. There is something in her face I have never seen before, though. Fear—that I won't care for her once she tells me the truth.

"I want to hear about your husband," I say.

Catherine tucks a piece of hair behind her ear, the way the Elizabeths do when it falls into their face. "He wasn't a bad man. In fact, he was probably better than most when he wasn't drinking. He didn't drink often, which was good because he was mean then."

She pauses and picks at the fringes of her shawl. "I thought he was dull and plain. He was a plodder. I thought he wasn't good enough for someone like me. I was very, very proud in those days, Charlotte. I had plans for myself, and I resented it when my father made me marry my husband."

"What is his name?" I ask.

"William Jones," Catherine says. "I have not said his name aloud for a very long time."

She pauses a moment, then goes on. "William gave me two children, but he did not give me the other things I wanted. So I found someone else who did. His name I will not speak. Ever.

"My husband had been drinking the night he found out. He came home, roaring and wild, and when I would not deny the truth of what he'd said, when I would not cry or grovel or beg for his forgiveness, he grabbed a hot poker and branded my face."

Catherine lifts a hand to touch her angry red scar.

"I left. I never went back. I made my way to Liverpool, where I kept myself in all the ways a woman can keep herself. There are many ways to keep yourself from starving, Charlotte. I pray you never have to discover them."

Overhead the stars burn brighter and brighter.

"Eventually I earned a reputation as a fine seamstress. And then one afternoon, I heard the missionaries preaching on a street corner. One of them was your John's uncle, Richard Bowen. They told me their stories and I laughed in their faces. Imagine! Strange angels. Golden plates. Outrageous. Still, I read their pamphlets. I read their ridiculous book. And something happened."

I turn to look at Catherine and see that her cheeks are shining with tears.

"The spirit touched my proud heart. And I believed," says Catherine. She looks up at the sky with a sad wondering smile. "I think God must laugh every time he thinks of it."

The breeze rustles through the grasses and branches.

"So now you know the worst there is to know about me," says Catherine. "Few people do. The Bowens. The elders who baptized me. And now you."

I shift Rose to one arm, and with the other I reach for

Catherine and pull her hard to me. I bury my face in her hair and I whisper fiercely, "Catherine Jones."

Catherine wraps her arms around me and Rose and holds us.

She smooths back my hair, takes my face between her hands, and kisses me on the forehead.

Rose laughs. Catherine and I look at each other, surprised. It's Rose's very first laugh!

We laugh, too.

"Well, well," says Catherine, "she's becoming her own little person now."

I nod.

"The first time is always a little miracle," says Catherine. "I remember very clearly the times my own children laughed." She pauses. "My son is your age, Charlotte. His name is Benjamin. My daughter is younger."

"What's your daughter's name?" I ask.

Catherine smiles. "Elizabeth."

I laugh.

"You remind me of her. In fact, when I first saw you on the ship, I couldn't stop staring at you."

Catherine looks at the stars and pulls her shawl tighter.

"I don't suppose I will ever see her again in this life, Charlotte, but if I do, it would please me to learn that she has something of your courage and of your grace."

I look at this strange and sad and beautiful woman sitting next to me.

Thank you, God, for giving me this friend.

"When tomorrow comes, I trust you to do the thing that's best for Rose," Catherine says. "Just as you have always done."

"Mostly done," I whisper.

Catherine stands and touches the top of my head. Then she lifts her skirts and walks away to the music of the trees.

· *Valley* ·

Thursday, October 2, 1856

❧

AT THE MOUTH OF EMIGRATION CANYON, UTAH

This morning I comb Rose's hair.

I wash her hands.

I wash her face.

I slip my necklace of beads over my head and wind it around and around her wrist.

I wrap her tight in Mam's yellow quilt, which I hope she will always keep and remember me by. Even if we do not see each other again in this life.

Then, flanked by Catherine Jones, Margaret Bowen, Lititia Roberts, Rosa Jenkins, and Ellenor Lewis, I find Thomas Owen, who is making final preparations for the day.

"Charlotte," he greets me with a shy smile. He nods at the other sisters behind me.

"I've brought you your daughter this morning, Brother Owen," I say.

Slowly, he stretches out his arms, which are as stiff as two boards.

I can't help myself. I just have to look at Sister Bowen, who grins and winks at me.

"Excuse me, Brother Owen, but a baby will roll right off arms like those." I laugh at him and so do my sisters.

Brother Owen blushes a little. "I would be most grateful to you, then, Sister Edwards, if you would show me how to hold my daughter."

"Bend your elbows."

He bends his elbows.

"And relax."

He tries.

"That's better. Don't be afraid, Brother Owen. Your daughter is not as fragile as she looks."

I lay Rose in her father's arms.

Thomas Owen looks at Rose. Then he pulls her close.

"What's her name, Charlotte?"

Her name? Her name is Rose. Rose beautiful and Rose rare. Rose bright and Rose fair. Rose red and Rose white. Rose of the prairies and of the mountains and of the desert valley, where she will blossom like a rose without me. Rose of my heart.

Charlotte's Rose.

I pause.

"She doesn't have one. She's been waiting for a father's name and for a father's blessing."

I cannot believe how strong my voice sounds.

Thomas Owen nods at me, then looks down at the bundle in his arms. He touches the tip of Rose's nose with his finger and smiles. "My daughter's name is Mary, then. After her mother, whom I love."

The sisters murmur their approval behind me. Then Sister Bowen steps forward and demonstrates the proper way to carry a baby in a sling. But not until she has squeezed my shoulder first.

The other women crowd around him, too, fussing and laughing. Only I stay rooted to the same spot.

Goodbye, Rose. Goodbye.

When the women finish with their business, they leave. Except for Catherine, who stands next to me.

Brother Owen's eyes find my face. He steps forward. "This noble thing you have done will never be forgotten, Sister Edwards." He removes his hat and kisses me on the cheek. His face is wet.

Then he and Mary leave.

"Well done, Charlotte," Catherine says in a low voice. She reaches for my hand, folds it up in her own, kisses the tips of my fingers. One by one by one.

John falls in beside me as I push the handcart.

"Let me help you," he says.

I don't feel like fighting with him, so I slide over. Besides, it'll feel good to have his arm rub up against mine. Already I miss the weight of Rose upon my back.

John and I don't speak. We just shove the handcart and breathe in time like oxen. I think of how hard the pushing was those first few weeks, when our Welsh skin was fair and we had no handcart muscles. I remember the tender blisters on my hands and on my feet.

But I also think of prairie scent after a rainstorm. Black soil perfume. I'm glad I have smelled it.

"Thank you," I say finally. I grin a little. "Even though I don't really need your help now. It was harder with Rose. Especially at first. But then I got used to her on my back."

John steals a quick glance at me. My face must say that I am all right, because he laughs. Oh, I do like that sound.

"So, John, do you still think I am a child?"

He knits together his thick black brows. "A child?"

"That's what you called me yesterday," I say. "Before I slapped you."

John touches the side of his face and grins. "I said you were a thirteen-year-old girl. That is not saying you are a child."

I shoot him a sideways glance. "You're being slippery with me, John Bowen. How is a thirteen-year-old girl different from a child?"

"A thirteen-year-old girl can take care of a baby, for one thing," he says.

"Yes," I whisper.

The handcart bumps over a patch of rocks. Pans rattle.

"All I meant yesterday is that you are still young," John says. "But no one could have taken better care of Rose than you did. Everyone says so."

I swallow hard and blink.

That makes me a woman now. Not a girl.

I almost say this to John but think better of it. One thing I am learning is that sometimes it doesn't matter what people think of you, even the people you love. And here's another: You don't have to say a thing aloud to make it real.

Or to make it true.

The sun sits straight up and yellow in the sky. Noon. We have reached the trail that winds down into the valley. The grown-ups stand in little groups and gossip. The children chase one another around and around like puppies nipping heels. Everyone is humming. Everyone is buzzing.

"Isn't it grand, Charlotte?" John asks. "Salt Lake at last! Perhaps Brother Brigham will ride up the mountainside on a white horse to greet us."

I laugh. "Wearing a top hat and waistcoat."

"Followed by all his wives!"

"What a sight that would be," I say.

John lets out a whoop and does a backflip, which sends his hat flying. I laugh until my sides ache.

After all these months.
Salt Lake City!
Zion.

Thomas and Mary Owen have already descended the trail into the valley. The rest of us are preparing to do so now. We yell at one another. We cheer for one another. When it is Catherine's turn, she reaches into her handcart and gives me her journal. Then she walks to the head of the trail, stops, and turns.

"When Brother Bowen and Brother MacDonald found me in Liverpool, I felt hope for the first time in a very long time. Only, I had nothing to offer God in return for noticing me again. 'God wants nothing from you but a broken and contrite heart,' those missionaries told me."

Now Catherine looks up, and though the sun beats down upon her face, she does not close her eyes or flinch.

"So. God. After much sorrow and even more sin, I offer you a contrite heart. A humble heart. But it is not broken. My spirit is not broken and will never be broken! I give you instead a stout and loyal heart. It is yours, God, to do with what you wish."

Catherine looks at us again.

"Thank you, my friends, for making me one of this community." Then Catherine Jones turns, gives her handcart a shove, and sends it crashing down the mountainside.

It smashes and splinters into a hundred pieces.

I gasp.

"Now!" shouts Catherine. "I enter my new life as I entered my old one. With no possessions to my name! With nothing but my stout heart!"

Catherine flings back her head and strides like a queen down the trail.

We are all in shock, I think, except for Papa. He has a look on his face that I have not seen since Mam was alive. And he is smiling.

All at once, the rest of us are cheering and roaring with laughter and stamping our feet because Catherine has smashed her handcart. We are throwing our hats and our bonnets into the air, and we are whooping like big bright angels.

Hosannah! Hosannah! Hosannah!

Oh, I will never forget this—the sight of all these hats floating in the sky. Nor will I forget the sound of these great ageless rocks ringing with our joyful noise.

So Papa and I watch as our friends walk, one by one, down the mountainside.

Ellenor Lewis. "I'm on my way to Salt Lake City to buy myself a nice pair of shoes."

Elias Lewis. "I will see that she doesn't lose them this time."

Rosa Jenkins with George on her hip.

Lititia Roberts with Emma in her arms.

Nathaniel Roberts still looking full of starch. Only not as full as he used to.

Margaret Bowen.

James Bowen. "After you, Daniel," says Brother Bowen to Papa with a sweeping bow.

"After you, James," Papa says back. "I insist!"

John. "A new beginning for all of us!" he says. And then he lifts me up and swings me round, laughing. He sets me back on my feet and runs down the trail.

"Ready, Charlotte?" Papa asks when our turn comes.

"Almost," I say. "I just want to remember how this moment looks so I can tell my babies about it someday."

As I stand here on the canyon rim, looking down this winding trail, I think of what Thomas Owen said this morning with his daughter, Mary, in his arms. *This noble thing you have done will never be forgotten.*

Maybe he won't forget. Truly, I hope he does not.

You never know.

But I will not forget. Not even if I live long enough to see this sky shatter into a thousand bright pieces and these mountains crumble into dust and the faraway seas swallow themselves dry.

I will remember what I have done.

I will remember my Rose.

God willing, I will write about her someday, too.

I draw a deep, deep breath. And then I take my first steps into the valley of the Great Salt Lake as Welsh voices rise up around me in song.

A Letter to the Reader

Brigham Young and his followers were determined to gather all their European brothers and sisters in Utah, even if those members of the church could not pay for the journey themselves. And many could not.

Nineteenth-century Mormonism, with its emphasis on social equality and communal living, had a special appeal for Europe's poor, who suffered under rigid class systems favoring the rich and powerful. For this purpose, the Perpetual Emigrating Fund was established—to outfit emigrants like Charlotte and Papa and assist them in reaching Zion.

Economic reverses in the territory of Utah during the 1850s, however, strapped the church's resources. Brigham Young therefore conceived of a radical plan to cut costs while providing European church members with an opportunity to emigrate to America. Nothing like it had been tried before: Emigrants would pull their own small wagons across prairies and over mountains to reach their new home.

And thus the handcart was born.

Between the years 1856 and 1860, ten handcart companies arrived in Utah. The third, Charlotte's company, left Iowa City on June 28, 1856, and arrived in Salt Lake City on October 2, 1856. It was made up primarily of church members from Wales. An American named Edward Bunker—seasoned pioneer, settler, missionary, and soldier—acted as their captain.

About the journey, Bunker wrote this in his brief autobiography: "The Welsh had no experience at all and very few of them could speak English. This made my burden very heavy. I had the mule team to drive and had to instruct the teamsters about yoking the oxen. The journey from the Missouri River to Salt Lake City was accomplished in 65 days. We were short of provisions all the way."

Although most of this novel's characters are ficitional, Bunker was a real person. So were Elias and Ellenor Lewis (who really did leave her shoes on the banks of the Missouri River and walk barefoot to Utah!). Other historical characters include two from the *S. Curling*—Elder Dan Jones and the blind harpist Thomas Giles, whose harp is on display at the Daughters of the Utah Pioneers museum in Salt Lake City. And of course, Brigham Young and Joseph Smith were real people, too.

The Rocky Mountain region the pioneers settled is a

very different place now than it was in the nineteenth century. It is not populated exclusively by Mormons but is home to people of all faiths. Nor do today's Mormons practice polygamy, a type of marriage that was officially discontinued by the church in 1890.

I learned about these people and the time in which they lived by reading primary and secondary sources that preserve details about the settlers' everyday lives. I also relied on the stories that I, a descendant of Mormon pioneers, have heard since I was a child: my grandmother's story about her own mother, whose family in England cut her off when she became a Mormon. Bessie Moon's story about her pioneer grandmother, who took her babies and wandered away from camp to die one desperate night. Ethella Berry's story about a stern Scotswoman named Margaret Douglish, who smashed her handcart as she looked down upon the Salt Lake valley for the first time and declared that the only possession she would keep was her "stout heart." Kathy Barnson's story about her ancestor, a survivor of the tragic Willie and Martin handcart companies, who kept putting one foot in front of the other, following a woman in white that only she could see. And, finally, Becky Thomas's story about a young girl who carried a baby on her back to Utah.

Like Charlotte, you have stories of your own. Funny ones, sad ones, dramatic ones. Treasure them and remember them. Write them down in a diary as Catherine

Jones did so that years and years from now your great-grandchildren will know who you were.

Your stories will matter in the future because you matter now.

And so I say goodbye to Charlotte. Whenever I think of her, I will remember the people who inspired me while writing this book.

Wendy Lamb, my friend and editor, who insisted that I look to my unique heritage and there find a tale to tell.

Pat Edwards, my mother, who told me to listen to Wendy.

Robert Kirby, columnist for *The Salt Lake Tribune*, who provided me with invaluable information on Wales, as well as on the third handcart company's sea voyage.

William W. Slaughter, a historian for the Church of Jesus Christ of Latter-day Saints and co-author of *Trail of Hope: The Story of the Mormon Trail*, who checked the manuscript for historical accuracy. Any factual errors in the novel are mine, not his.

Ken Cannon, my husband, whose extensive knowledge of and passion for Mormon history has rubbed off on me.

Finally, I will always remember Emma Thomas and how she started the whole thing.

Just by being Emma.

A. E. Cannon
October 2001

· ABOUT THE AUTHOR ·

A. E. Cannon has written a number of books for young readers, including *Cal Cameron by Day, Spider-Man by Night* (Winner of the Delacorte Press Prize for a First Young Adult Novel), *The Shadow Brothers* (an ABA Pick of the Lists), and *Amazing Gracie* (an ALA choice as one of the best 100 books for young adult readers during the past twenty years). A. E. Cannon resides in Salt Lake City, where she is a columnist for the *Deseret News*. She lives with her husband, Ken, and their five sons.